About the Author

Jonathan Phoinex worked in emergency services for almost two decades. He was a second-generation fire fighter following in his father's footsteps when he turned eighteen. He was a certified IFSAC (International Fire Service Accreditation Congress) Fire Instructor, a 911 Dispatcher and certified Emergency Medical Technician. He left active service several years ago due to his struggle with PTSD but still supports local departments however he can. He now lives in the South Carolina Low Country with his spouse and two children. He currently attends Purdue Global University, where he is completing his Bachelor's in Emergency Management.

Through the Flames

Jonathan Phoinex

Through the Flames

Olympia Publishers
London

www.olympiapublishers.com
OLYMPIA PAPERBACK EDITION

A CIP catalogue record for this title is
available from the British Library.

ISBN: 978-1-80074-157-7

This is a work of fiction.
Names, characters, places and incidents originate from the writer's
imagination. Any resemblance to actual persons, living or dead, is
purely coincidental.

First Published in 2021

Olympia Publishers
Tallis House
2 Tallis Street
London
EC4Y 0AB

Printed in Great Britain

Dedication

This book is dedicated to the men and women of the fire service, who daily give so much of themselves to protect others. Thank you.

Prologue

On a cold autumn morning, a parade of fire trucks travelled down South Live Oak Drive preceded by a guard of six motorcycle police officers. The lead engine, Engine 212, was draped with black cloth and a black wreath at its front. Standing on the tailboard, firefighters in dress uniform clung to the rear of the truck while behind it, the rest of Company 21 marched, followed closely by a dozen trucks from different departments, law enforcement officers and then, family and friends. This was the last ride of Assistant Chief William P. Miller.

At the entrance to the cemetery, two ladder trucks sat, their ladders extended and a large American flag hung between them over the entrance, awaiting the engine to drive under. The motorcycle officers took position on either side of the entrance, allowing Engine 212 to lead the procession to its final destination. It proceeded through the large cemetery lined with grand, live oaks, moss hanging from their branches, to a plot near the back where a large, open tent sat with several chairs set up. Floral wreaths sat on either side of the gravesite and at their centre, was a picture of the former chief in a blue fire department T-shirt standing next to the engine that carried him here. From the smile he had, the large man seemed full of happiness, his cheeks rosy, his brown hair sticking out under his cap and his eyes full of hope. At the bottom was a small plaque reading, 'Captain Miller 10-12-1995 with Engine 212'.

As the procession came to a stop, the fire chief in dress

whites guided Engine 212 into position near the gravesite. He directed several other firefighters in uniform lineup, creating a corridor leading from the tailboard of the truck to the site itself. Finally, the officer driving the truck stepped down from the cab. He straightened his uniform and placed a captain's cover on his closely-shaved head. He was almost the spitting image of the man pictured next to the firetruck twenty years before.

He was quickly joined by two other firefighters in dress uniforms. The first was Frankie Casselman, the captain's best friend. He was slightly slimmer, his hair cut high and tight, his blue eyes standing out against his tanned skin. The second was Kayla Lee. She was slightly taller than the two of them with brunette hair pulled up into a bun. Together, they made their way to the back of the truck, joining the other firefighters there.

Captain Miller took a few steps from the truck, allowing for the other pallbearers to take their positions before belting out, "Company, attention!" The gathered officers snapped to attention and the casket was lowered from the hose bed, by the two firefighters riding the tailboard and its pallbearers. Once down, the captain gave a shout: "Present arms!" The assembled in uniform all saluted as the casket, draped in a flag of Station 21, was carried to the gravesite. They stood motionless but on the faces of many, the pain and sorrow were undeniable. Captain Miller marched in front, leading them the last few yards before stopping and saluting while the casket was set down. Once the casket was in position, the officers who bore its weight stepped back and saluted it, waiting on their next order. "At ease!" the captain bellowed, before turning to sit in an empty seat reserved for family.

As the chief walked up to the small podium to prepare for the ceremony, he cleared his throat, then spoke; his tone even and calm. "Since its conception, the fire service has been closely related to the ringing of bells   . In the past, a bell would signal the start of a firefighter's shift. During the day, it was a bell that would signal to the firefighter the need for his service to protect the lives of the citizens under his care and when the call was done, it was the bell that signalled the completion of the call and the time to return home. Today, we still hold true to these traditions as a symbol of honour and respect to those who have given so much of themselves and who served the public proudly. We symbolise the devotion that these brave souls had for their duty with a special signal: three rings, three times each, representing the end of their duties and that they are returning to quarters, their tasks completed and their duties well done. This, their final alarm, signals that they are returning home."

Once he finished speaking, the bell chimed three times, then three again and then three once more. Suddenly, a tone rang out as the radios on every firefighter began to sound off. The static on the radio cracked and a voice called out, "Twenty-one oh two, twenty-one oh two, twenty-one oh two, Central to all units, end of watch for Assistant Chief William Miller. Twenty-one oh two is out of service and has gone home." Many of the firefighters began to cry as a bagpipe played 'Amazing Grace' in the distance. The colour guard stepped forward and folded the flag, before presenting it to the seated family and saluting the captain. The chief at the podium saluted the casket then bellowed, "Detail, dismissed," and the assembled fire fighters began to move away from the grave site.

One officer didn't move. He sat in his seat, staring through his dark glasses at the casket.

"Captain Miller," a voice broke him from his thoughts. He looked up to see the chief standing before him.

"Chief Rose, thank you for taking over for me." He looked back at the casket.

"Of course, son. May I sit?" He sat next to the young captain as he nodded.

"Your father was a good man, Wayne and a good friend. He made this department proud," he said, staring forward, "but you were the one thing that made him the proudest."

A small smile hit Captain Miller's face. "He used to say I was the only one of his sons he still had to put up with at home."

Chief Rose nodded, "He embraced the idea that we were one big family and replacing him will be a tall order for anyone who tries to but if anybody could do it, you could."

Captain Miller looked confused. "Sir, are you offering me my father's job? What about the battalion chief?"

Chief Rose nodded, "Barry is two years from retirement if not sooner and isn't interested in the position. Letting you skip a step was his idea but I don't think it was a bad idea. Take your leave and think about it, son. It'll be here when you get back, if you want it. It's what he would have wanted, I think."

The chief stood, saluted once more, then turned and shook the captain's hand before leaving the grave site, leaving the son alone with his father and his thoughts. It was at this moment, while others were chatting and saying their goodbyes, that he finally allowed himself the moment to cry.

Chapter 1

The old Hyperion Technologies Building was ablaze, flames shooting high above its three-storey frame. It stood on the edge of the lake and the reflection in the dark water at night was eerie and frightening. The glow from the inferno illuminated the surrounding grounds, making it seem like daylight as the firefighters scrambled to battle the blaze.

Captain Miller stood in front of Engine 210 staring at the inferno that had engulfed the southwest corner of the Old Jefferies Building. "All units report in," he said into the radio on his shoulder.

"Attack One, we're on the first floor have confirmed fire near the A-B corner," a voice crackled from the radio.

"Rescue Team One exiting from the second floor with two P.I.s, advise medical," came another response.

"Rescue Team Two, we're approaching the C-D corner on floor one, continuing search," was the final transmission.

Captain Miller turned towards the ambulance crew waiting nearby. "I got two patients coming out the main entrance, probably gonna need O_2." As more trucks arrived, Captain Miller continued to shout orders, "Have the Two-Six take the A side and protect that exposure. Get me an ETA on additional medic units. Have Seven-One prep their Ritt team, so Fifty-four can stand down."

He was calm, even though the urgency in his speech was apparent. He knew his men; he knew his neighbouring stations and they knew their jobs. So long as they worked together, this was something they could handle. The older trucks that were arriving reminded him of how far things had come since he first set foot in a fire house.

Wayne Miller had been doing this all his life it seemed. When he was twelve, his father took him to the firehouse for the first time. Back then, the department was much smaller, working out of a small sixty by eighty-foot garage, basically. The department was all volunteer and had two engines: Engine 210, which was a 1969 Ford front-end pumper with a seven-hundred-and-fifty-gallon tank and Engine 211, a 1983 American Lafrance Cab-over with a thousand-gallon tank. The two old trucks required a lot of maintenance and he spent many Saturdays at the station with his father and the other firefighters, working on the trucks. When they weren't working on the trucks, the chief at the time would do things like challenge him to roll hose faster or race him across the hose bed of Engine 211.

In those days, his father wouldn't let him near a charged line but he let him learn how to work the pump. He taught him how to throttle the engine and what valves started to move the water properly through the pump. His father taught him about friction loss and water hammer and the effects it had, not just on the truck but on the firefighters at the end of the line.

By sixteen, Wayne was officially considered a junior firefighter and had his own gear and helmet. His father was now the safety captain and though he didn't allow Wayne to fight fire, he did let him train with the other firefighters. He could hoist a ladder and tie a bowline; he could name all of the tools on the truck and knew their purpose. He would often invite his best friend to join him but the offer was always turned down.

When he was eighteen, Wayne had a huge falling out with his father. He moved to Myrtle Beach for a few months and worked on the strip as a security guard. Meanwhile, his best friend Frankie joined the Marine Corps and he left for Parris

Island. It took three months before Wayne decided to come home and his father welcomed him with open arms. Wayne went to school and started working for an electrician. But the fire department called to him and it wasn't long before he made his way to the academy.

Captain Miller was directing external support operations when Lt. Mellon ran to him from the building, bringing him out of his trip down memory lane. "Cap, she's breathing from the sides," he yelled as he pointed to the building on fire, "I think she's about to go."

As he looked, he saw smoke leaking from the walls on the A-B corner of the building and he heard creaking and snapping, now coming from the structure. He knew there was no saving the building any longer and it could collapse at any time.

He grabbed the nearest radio. "Emergency Traffic, all crews evacuate now. I repeat, evacuate now," he shouted into the radio, then turned, "Sound evacuation, pull the teams back and get me a count." Lt. Mellon jumped into the cab of a nearby engine and laid on the air horn. Other apparatus joined in, sounding their sirens and air horns for a full minute, as firefighters scrambled from the building. They all knew the universal signal to drop everything and go meant they were in danger.

For a moment, Wayne was reminded of his class A burn back at the academy. He was leading the primary rescue team into the building performing a right-side search, while the attack team proceeded to the base of the fire. After searching several rooms, they found a stairway leading upstairs and could hear an alarm going off from a personal alert safety system or P.A.S.S device. Wayne proceeded to the top of the stairs where they found their victim lying and called for his team. They grabbed her and began to carry her when the ladder team opened a side window not far from them and began to make entry. Not wanting to waste time, Wayne took the patient to them to extricate her and led his team

15

to continue their search.

When they came out, Wayne was proud of how they performed; the lead instructor was not. Wayne's team had been instructed to perform a search on floor one. By leaving the first floor they put themselves in danger because command wouldn't know to search the second floor for them. It was the first time Wayne had heard the term 'freelancing': performing actions outside of commands ordered and after the thorough dressing down, it was something he would never forget. He had three more runs that day, as the attack team, rapid intervention team and ladder team, so he followed orders perfectly for them. On that day, he realised the importance of working as a team and the chain of command; a lesson that stuck with him his whole career.

Wayne began asking the different commanders to confirm they had got everyone out. He was on his way to his engine when it happened. The sound was deafening as the corner closest to the seat of the fire collapsed into the building. The dust cloud billowed out towards him and he shielded his face for a moment, before viewing what was left. The corner the attack team was working in was down to a single storey, flames now barely visible as the debris had partially smothered them. On the opposite side of the building the second and third floors had partially survived. From his position, Wayne wasn't sure how much of the first floor could possibly still exist, there was no hope of any further internal operations from the looks of it.

He approached his crew, prepared to start issuing orders when he noticed someone was missing. "Where's Frank and Lee?" he asked Mellon. Mellon was staring at the building in silence and it was then Wayne realised what that meant. Somewhere inside the remains of that building were two firefighters who had trusted him to get them home safe. He thought of every possible scenario he could remember, his mind going a mile a minute. Someone had to go in and get them out.

The captain took a single deep breath, the world around him slowed as he processed what he needed to do next. He closed his eyes and pictured the layout of the building from the pre-planning they had done and tried to place where his firefighters might have been heading and what they could be near to. He opened his eyes and grabbed a set of some of the heavy extrication tools.

"Mellon, we're going around back to try and access that side of the building from the emergency corridor." His eyes focused on the far corner where he knew an emergency exit was. "Take over command of operations here and send me a second crew back there with a K12 and air tool, in case we gotta cut the concrete."

The Lieutenant nodded, proceeded towards the main engine and Captain Miller and the rest of their crew proceeded to the back of the structure. The side of the building here looked intact from the outside but Wayne knew from experience that it didn't mean the inside was in the same shape. As he arrived at the emergency door, another firefighter rushed forward with a Kelly Bar and began to pry the door open.

It took only a few minutes to open the door; inside was dark and cloudy with dust and smoke. The plans of the building showed this corridor ran the length of this side of the building and with only a few doors along it, leading into the building proper. Wayne knelt down and pulled his mask over his head then covered it with his flash hood and helmet.

"Mask up people, we only got one shot," he shouted, before connecting his regulator and running into the black expanse.

Chapter 2

Inside the abandoned power station, Frankie Casselman crawled along the outside wall reaching out to feel if he could find anybody in the darkness. He had almost no visibility, as the light on his helmet barely illuminated a few feet ahead of him. Behind him, Kayla Lee kept one hand on his ankle as she reached out with a halogen bar, trying to make contact with anybody who may be there, yet hoping that everyone was already out by now.

"Fire Department," she would shout. "Call out if you can hear me," and Frankie would follow suit.

"Fire Department, he'd yell. "Is anybody here?"

Their calls remained unanswered as they continued along the C side of the building, slowly moving away from the source of the fire. As they cleared each room, they'd mark the door and continue on to the next office. The heat had been intense and the longer they searched, the more they worried that if they found anyone it would be less of a rescue and more of a body recovery.

The structure around them creaked and moaned as the fire raged behind them. They passed through a concrete fire wall that had yet to be breached and shut the door behind them, knowing there was a way out ahead. This area was less smokey but still dark. They were able to see more and began to separate a little, in order to search faster. Frankie entered a bathroom near the corner of the building leaving Kayla at the door while he searched; they used a rope to stay connected so as not to lose each other.

The sound of the building creaking began to get louder. Kayla tugged twice on the rope, signalling to Frankie.

"It's not gonna hold much longer, we need to get out," she yelled, over the sounds of chaos around her. Frankie nodded and began to make his way back out. The sound of sirens began to echo from far off.

"Shit!" Frankie exclaimed, he grabbed his partner and began to run towards the exit.

"We gotta evac. now!"

They ran for the door to the emergency corridor. From there he thought, a secondary exit shouldn't be far. The building's moaning became louder, Kayla shoved Frankie into a small office just as the building began to crumble around them. He tumbled, his radio and helmet flying off as he went down, striking his head; then everything went black.

The dust was thick and it was quiet, when he came to some time later. He could hear Kayla's P.A.S.S. device screaming, letting him know she had not moved for at least a minute. He made his way towards the sound just inside the door. He found her underneath some ceiling tiles and a lighting fixture that had struck her as she drove them both in here. The door they'd come in was blocked with debris.

Frankie cleared the debris from over Kayla and began to check her for injuries. Satisfied she wasn't badly hurt, he tried to rouse her.

"Hey, Lee, can you hear me?" he said, while tapping her shoulder. She replied with a groan of pain and began to move.

"I feel like I got hit by a truck." She started to lift herself up slowly and looked behind her where they had been running. "Wasn't that our way out?"

Frankie nodded and tried to think where they might be in the building. He knew they were near an outside wall but that was probably a foot-thick concrete, the wall behind them could be supporting debris and if compromised, it might make their situation worse. If they were near the emergency corridor, they could try and breach that wall. It would only be about six inches thick but there was no guarantee it wasn't steel reinforced concrete as well and they had no tools to get through that.

When he left the Marine corps, Frankie found himself with a lot of free time on his hands. He had saved for four years while he served his country and he bought a small place on the river and Wayne had moved in with him. Wayne had been working for the fire department for three years by then and was preparing for his engineers' test. Frankie, of course, was constantly forced to help him study. Occasionally, they would get help from Scott Mellon. He had just passed the engineers' exam and knew every truck pretty much back and forward. Scott had been dating a young bartender whose name Frankie couldn't remember but it was through her, that they had found Kayla and soon she was around more than Scott was.

That was the start of the friendship between them; a bond that transferred over to the fire station when Kayla and eventually, Frankie joined. It was this bond that made them such a good team; they weren't just co-workers, they were a family. Frankie knew that no matter what, Wayne and Scott were coming for them. They just needed to figure out which way they were coming.

He picked up his Kelly Tool and made his way to the wall he suspected was shared with the emergency corridor. He used the tool and began tapping the wall to estimate the type of construction. It was definitely concrete. If he had a sledgehammer and maybe a couple of hours, he could probably knock a hole in it big enough to crawl out of. He didn't have either of those things and the effort would only use up the limited air supply quicker.

He sat down and began tapping the Kelly Bar on the wall in a repeating pattern, Tap-tap-tap, tap,tap,tap, tap-tap-tap. He would pause for a second or two then do it again. Kayla moved over to where he was, thinking he had given up.

"We're gonna get outta here, you can't give up," she said, shaking him.

He grinned, his blue eyes gleaming in the low light. "Who's giving up, I'm telling Wayne where to make the hole."

She looked from him to the wall and back to him for a moment. "You mean, that's the wall,"

He cut her off. "Yep, to the emergency corridor, it's reinforced and when I did the pre-plan, it was determined to be the best point to perform a rescue operation on the back side of the building."

Kayla began searching the room for something solid. She found a three-hole punch and began tapping the wall in the same pattern as Frankie. Inside the building, it was silent except for their tapping and the sound of their air packs. They tapped for several minutes, hearing nothing. Suddenly, they began to hear a loud scraping sound and they cleared away from the wall, ten minutes later and there was a hole barely big enough for someone's head to fit through. They could see lights shining from the other side. Two air tanks were slid through the hole, allowing them to replace their limited air supply, followed by a second Kelly Bar and a sledgehammer.

Kayla changed her air tank and then grabbed the sledge. "Typical, a modern woman's always gotta rescue herself," she joked and she began breaking the concrete around the hole to make it bigger. Frankie joined suit with the Kelly Bar and with both crews working from either side, they began widening the hole.

For fifteen minutes they chipped away concrete and cut steel until the hole was big enough for them to squeeze through and together, the crew of Station 21 made their way out of the building, just like Wayne had planned. As they emerged from the building, Frankie and Kayla happily removed their masks and got a breath of fresh air.

Wayne pulled off his mask and helmet. "You two get in the command truck, I'm taking you to get checked out," he said, motioning to Frankie and Kayla. Frankie went to protest but a quick look from the captain said that it would not even be considered.

On the opposite side of the building, Lt. Mellon had successfully led the operation to control the remains of the fire. He was in the process of releasing the mutual aid stations and setting up crews for overhaul. He saw the crew coming from the back side of the building.

"Captain," he called out, "while you guys were goofing off, we were out here working ya know." Wayne looked at him, grinned and laughed. "Well, damn Scott, looks like you're after my job, guess you can handle the rest from here, I'm taking these two to get checked."

Scott gave him a sly grin as Wayne jumped into the command truck with Frankie and Kayla. He breathed a sigh of relief as they drove off, then turned back to the task at hand. He had to get this scene wrapped up if he wanted any sleep tonight.

Chapter 3

As day broke, the smoke had mostly cleared over what remained of the Jefferies Power Station. A single vehicle remained on the scene, labelled Berkeley County Fire Marshal. Two figures sifted through some of the debris near where the fire seemed to have started. The first was Fire Marshal David Green, an older, black man of about average height with what most would consider a 'dad bod', his hair and moustache were mostly grey and the years of service were evident by the lines on his face. His assistant, Sylvia Branton, was much younger than her mentor, being only twenty-three years of age. She was small and slender with red hair and freckled skin. Her hard-rimmed glasses covered green eyes that shone like emeralds.

She was scraping a patch of burnt concrete on the floor of the rubble and placed the scrapings into a small tube. The clear liquid in the tube instantly reacted to the scrapings, turning a dark red colour. "Sir, look at this," she said, holding up the tube.

Marshal Green made his way to her. "Let's have a look, Kid." Kid was his pet-name for Sylvia. He took the tube and studied it for a few seconds before kneeling and scraping off a bit of the residue himself. He placed a bit on the tip of his finger, then smelled it and placed his finger just on the tip of his tongue. He stood silent for a minute, then made an offended face and spat out the material.

"Alcohol based, definitely an accelerant used, this confirms arson," he said, looking around at the destroyed building. "We need to get samples ready to be sent to the lab in Columbia and tell them we need them back asap." He began grabbing evidence bags and scraping around the spot. Sylvia paused for a second then asked a serious question. "This is just like the last two, isn't it David?"

David shook his head. "The last two fires were abandoned buildings, this one was occupied, that's an escalation kid."

An hour later they arrived at Station 21, Engine 210 and Ladder 21 were on the pad getting scrubbed down before the end of shift. Inside the bay, Captain Miller and several firefighters were practicing yoga for a morning workout. David noted that while he was much older than the captain, he definitely wasn't nearly that limber any more.

The inspectors waited patiently 'til they were done before getting the captain's attention. "Miller, quit showing off for the probies!"

Wayne made his way over and laughing, said, "David you're just jealous you can't move like I can."

David smiled widely. "From what your wife says I don't need to, guess it's all about the right equipment."

Wayne hugged his friend, laughing, "I don't have a comeback for that one so point goes to you."

Sylvia shook her head at them and stated in a very matter of fact tone, "I'll never understand why you men do that, especially when everyone knows it takes a woman to please a woman."

David and Wayne stared at her, their mouths agape for a moment as they processed the sly insult they had just received, then erupted in laughter, bringing a smile to the young Marshal's face. "David, she's more dangerous than you are," Wayne joked. "At this rate you need to look into early retirement."

David nodded. "She does always make me proud, one hell

of an investigator; speaking of which we need to talk."

Wayne nodded and led them to his office, offering them a seat. He grabbed a bottle of water from his mini-fridge and leaned on his desk in front of them. David handed him the report on the Jefferies fire. Highlighted on it was the line reading, '*unk accelerant possible alcohol based*'. He looked up at David and Sylvia, the concern evident on their faces. "Is it the same style and chemical as the other two?"

Sylvia glanced at David who nodded, then she presented her evidence. "The fire clearly started in a small, sealed room where an accelerant was used to allow it to build quickly. It's possible that additional fuel was stored there to allow it to spread faster as well. We located several trails that show the accelerant was placed to guide the fire to areas where it would find an ample fuel source." She paused for a second, then pulled out two folders and handed them to him. "These are the same patterns found at the fire at the abandoned Powertech factory and the old presbyterian church in the past month. Both of those buildings were abandoned for some time. Jefferies, even though it's shut down still had a small workforce onsite."

Wayne walked around to the back of his desk and sat in his chair, looking briefly at a photo on the wall of him, his father, Frankie and Kayla when she had graduated from the Academy. She was in the first class of recruits that he trained. He had just become lieutenant back then. Frankie had been in the department for maybe a year and his dad was still healthy. He had remembered his father saying how proud he was that all his kids were firefighters now. That was how he had looked at Frankie and Kayla, not just as young people who were friends with his son but as his own kids. Last night someone almost took their lives and it was intentional.

"Who else knows all this?" he asked, looking back at David and Sylvia. "Who do we need to bring in?"

"County has a Certified Fire investigator, April Wells, you know her, she was looking into the Powertech fire. At first, we figured it was an insurance scam but now…" he trailed off, almost as if what he thought was too dangerous to say. Sylvia cleared her throat then spoke, "Captain, in situations like this the first suspects that need to be ruled out are the responders in that area sir, it's possible that—"

Wayne slammed his fist on the table, cutting her off. "That's bullshit, every one of my crew went into those buildings and I almost lost two of them, now you wanna blame them!" His face was red with anger as he stood from his chair. Sylvia had never seen this side of him before and for a second, she was worried he was going to attack them.

David spoke calmly but avoided looking at Wayne, "Nobody thinks they did it but we have to question them. Maybe they saw something they didn't think was important but it was. We wanted to give you a fair warning before it started."

Wayne crossed his arms, the anger still very evident on his face. "Ask any question you need to, you can use my office but my team didn't do it. I'll call the crew back in but watch your ass or it'll be 03 all over again, David." He stormed out of the office and made his way towards the truck bay.

Sylvia turned towards David. "03?" she inquired.

David looked away as if ashamed. "I accused his father of trying to protect a possible arsonist, things got heated and Wayne put me on my ass."

Sylvia was shocked. Wayne was almost always happy and joking around, she would never have thought him to be violent. David gave a chuckle. "You wouldn't think he gets violent but

26

you go after one of his and he's like a demon. He's been willing to fight just as hard for me as anybody in this department. I really feel for the first guy who breaks his daughter's heart."

Officer Wells arrived about an hour later, she was around five feet eight with curly, dark hair, tanned skin and an athletic figure. She went to greet Wayne but the second she saw his face, she made a U-turn and went straight into the office without so much as a word to the captain. April had known him since high school and she knew he was very hard to anger but when you did, just avoid him. She was a former marine and nurse before she became a cop. She volunteered for the arson training because she thought she'd get to work closely with firefighters and so many of her friends were in the department. Unfortunately, when they saw her coming most times it wasn't a friendly visit and the conversations were far from enjoyable.

Over the next several hours, every firefighter from all three shifts at station 21 came in for an interview. For most of them it was their day off and they were annoyed to say the least. The last interview was Kayla Lee. She was bandaged from injuries she'd got during the collapse. April knew Kayla wasn't the type to set fires but she had to do her job. Kayla walked into the room in blue jean shorts and a halter top, her skin gleaming from a light bead of sweat from the South Carolina summer heat. She gave Sylvia a wry smile, causing her to nervously glance away momentarily, before sitting and glaring at April.

April pushed record on the device sitting between them, then cleared her throat.

"Firefighter Lee, are you aware why you are here?" she asked.

"Because you're a cop and the lead in your bullets fills your head sometimes?" Kayla quipped back sarcastically, before giving a real answer, "Cause you think one of us set that fire."

April nodded. "I don't think any of you did it but I have to rule you all out and I have to know what you saw." She tried to take as relaxed a stance as possible, so she wouldn't upset her any more than she was.

"How many times have you been to Jefferies in the last forty-eight hours?"

Kayla sighed in frustration then took a deep breath. "Once; I was on the first engine to respond to the fire last night."

'This is good.' April thought, 'she's less hostile, maybe she'll be easier to work with.' "Can you describe your initial response?"

Kayla groaned but answered, "It was a textbook response, Engine 210 took an attack position, Scott had the backup, lay a line in from the hydrant, Ladder 21 set on the A-D corner, we met with security, they said people were still inside, McMurray and Cambell were teamed up and me and Frankie of course, went in for Search and Rescue and Tillman and Watts had the attack line. We filled them in and searched left-side throughout the building 'til it came down on our heads."

April nodded, "Did you notice anything unusual?"

Kayla was about to snap 'no' when a thought hit her. "Me and Frankie pre-planned that building. Where we found the seat of the fire shouldn't have had anything that would've burned that hot, it was mainly the break area and cafeteria and most of that was shut down. I mean, it shouldn't have been enough to cause that spread or bring the place down so fast."

April and Sylvia exchanged a glance. "So that area was largely unused?"

Kayla nodded. "After they shut the main plant down, that area of the building was really only used for meetings. I mean, everybody was usually up in the control room or in the back offices where we got trapped."

April turned off the recorder and looked at Kayla. "Kayla, thank you. I'm sorry you had to come in here but we have to follow procedure." She reached out to shake Kayla's hand and for a moment, Kayla let it sit there before accepting it.

"Just make sure you catch whoever did this April and remember who your friends are." She walked out with the same swagger she walked in with, only briefly turning towards Sylvia to give her a wink before vanishing from sight.

"Sylvia you're drooling," April said flatly, gathering her papers and files, "though I guess I can see why but come on, I gotta face Wayne and he's easier to deal with when kids are around."

Chapter 4

It was a warm day in late spring, the smell of charcoal burning as the grill heated up, filled the air. Wayne exited his lake house carrying a large, aluminium pan filled with uncooked burgers, hot dog and ribs ready for the grill. Behind him, his son Adam followed with another pan containing the chicken leg quarters he'd help his father prepare. Adam at seventeen, was only half an inch shorter than his father, with long, dirty blonde hair and mild acne on his face, his chin showed a few hairs that had started to grow suggesting it was time he started shaving. He had thick-rimmed glasses and almost always wore khakis and a polo shirt, today's choice being salmon in colour; a contrast to the black and blue Hawaiian shirt his father was wearing with his khaki shorts.

They sat their pans on a table next to the large, brick grill that was in their backyard. Wayne, Frank and Adam had built it by hand several summers ago and whenever they had gatherings, it was Wayne's pride and joy to show off. Lifting the cover, a plume of smoke flew out momentarily engulfing the two, causing them to cough and wave their hands in front of their faces. "Geez Dad, are you trying to kill me?" the young man quipped after regaining his breath.

"No point in that, son," Wayne responded flatly, "we don't have enough insurance on you yet." He gave his son a wry smile and pointed to a box at the end of the table. "Get started on those decorations, everyone will be here soon for the party." Adam snapped to attention and gave a fake salute, "Aye, Aye, captain!"

before grabbing the box and heading to the back porch.

Wayne began placing the chicken on one side of the grill, grinning at the sound of meat sizzling. His wife, Crystal, emerged from the back door. She was much shorter than her husband and son, with a sultry, curved figure and long, flowing red hair. She wore blue jeans and a t-shirt with a BAU logo on it; Criminal Minds was her favourite show. She carried a large plate covered with tin foil and sat it on the table before wrapping her arms around her husband.

"Sometimes I think you love that grill more than me," she said, grinning at him. He leaned down and kissed her. "Never, the grill won't do what you did last night," he responded playfully.

She smacked his rear at the comment. "Careful hero, you'll be sleeping at work." She turned and went back inside, pausing to playfully smack her son before entering. Adam had successfully hung the banner that said 'Happy Birthday Dani' on it and was admiring his work. He was the first to hear the sound of the loud engine making its way down the road. "Uncle Frankie!" he exclaimed, before running around the front of the house.

Frankie drove a fully restored 1966 Camarro, though he told Adam it would be his if he graduated High School with a higher GPA than his. Currently, Frankie was suspecting he'd have to find a new car next year. It was cherry red with a white stripe down the centre, the loud, Chevy V8 had an unmistakable rumble as it approached the house. He pulled up, got out and then opened the door for his wife Rea and his young son Franklin. Rea and Frankie were almost the same height. She had dark brunette hair and glasses. She grabbed a car and led Franklin into the house, from which the loud excited greeting of, "Oh my god, it's so good to see you," and "he's got so big," could be heard from Crystal.

As Frankie shut the door and turned, Adam came charging from the back of the house launching himself at him. "Gotcha," he said, trying to grapple the older man, who swiftly dodged before putting Adam in a headlock. "You gotta try harder than that kid," he said before releasing him. "Where's your old man?" Adam motioned his head to the back yard. "The captain is on the grill," he said jokingly, "but how's my car?" He looked at it as if he was inspecting it for damage. "Is it still running good, did you check the timing like I said? Are we gonna install NOS?" Frankie shook his head at the rapid-fire questions. "Yes, yes, no, your father would kill us both and it's not your car until you graduate kiddo," Frankie replied.

"Don't worry Uncle Frankie, I'm gonna beat you," he said, leading him to the back yard where Wayne was now adding the hamburgers to the grill. He was pleased to discover they were both wearing the Hawaiian shirt and khaki combo. "Hey loser, I see great mind think alike," he called to his best friend.

"Shut up and help me not burn this meat," Wayne replied, reaching into a cooler and grabbing a beer to offer him. He popped the top and the two toasted.

"So, where's the birthday girl, Buddy Boy." Frankie was looking around but there was no sign of Wayne's daughter.

Wayne motioned over his shoulder. "Crystal's mom and sister took her out today so we could surprise her with all this, she should be back in a little bit so hopefully people hurry up and get here." Frankie nodded and the two continued to chit chat as Adam, Crystal and Rea continued setting up tables and decorating and Franklin played in the yard, with Wayne's large German Shepherd, Chief.

Gradually over the next thirty minutes the party goers arrived, David Green with his son, Michael, who immediately went with Adam to play Smash Brothers. Kayla by herself who grabbed a drink and joined the ladies giggling in the shade. Scott Mellon with his wife, Tonya and their son, Malik. He was in the same class as Danni and rumoured to have got into a fight in her defence on more than one occasion. Several parents dropped off Danni's friends and said they'd be back after the party.

When Crystal's sister pulled up with her mother and Danni, everyone got quiet waiting for Danni to come around back, before yelling, 'Surprise'. Danni was almost her mother's height at just under five feet, with short hair and glasses. She was a bit of a tomboy in a blue jean jumper with a yellow striped t-shirt. She smiled widely as her friends all ran to her to hug her. Somebody turned on the stereo and immediately Kayla was leading a group of thirteen-year-old girls, in dances like the Electric Slide and the Macarena.

A blue van pulled into the driveway and a young woman got out of the vehicle and walked around to open the sliding door. She was slender with curly, dark hair and tanned skin. She wore short shorts and a moderately-covering crop top. She pulled a wheelchair out of her van and then helped a young boy get into it and got an O_2 canister out for him as well. She started to wheel him up the driveway when Crystal noticed them and ran over. "Oh Joyce, I'm glad you could make it, everyone's around back."

She led them to where the party goers were gathered and called Danni to her. "Danni this is Timmy and his mom Joyce. He wanted to join you and your friends today."

Danni was a very accepting child and without so much as a breath, grabbed the chair and started to push him towards her friends. "Sure," she said, before calling to her friends, "Hey Jenna, come help me with Timmy." A young girl came and together they got him to the table where she and her friends were.

Joyce smiled and turned to Crystal. "Thank you so much for inviting us, Timmy hasn't had a chance to make any new friends since we moved here." Wayne walked over to them. "Ms. Carson, I didn't know you were coming, how are you?" He looked from her to Crystal and Crystal spoke up, "Joyce and I met when she brought Timmy to the station to see the fire trucks and I thought it would be nice for him to come and join in."

Wayne smiled. Joyce had brought Timmy to the station several times. He always seemed to enjoy the fire trucks but he couldn't help being a little disconcerted by this sudden breach from the station coming into his home life. Still, he was a gracious host and the young boy didn't have any friends so he accepted that Crystal knew better than he did.

"Of course, the more the merrier. I hope you like hamburgers 'cause I made plenty. There's also chicken and hotdogs."

Joyce smiled gratefully. "Thank you so much Captain Miller, you all are so nice." She walked over to check on her son and Wayne watched carefully. He was always cautious when new people were around.

Crystal pulled him aside. "She seems nice but I'm more concerned about her son."

Wayne looked puzzled for a moment, then looked back at the boy sitting in a wheelchair having fun. "Timmy's a good kid, he's had it rough, he was almost killed in a fire that killed his father," he said, not sure what concern she could have about the young boy.

"Wayne, I'm not concerned about him, I'm concerned *for* him. I don't think she'd hurt him, at least I hope not but it can't be healthy for them to be isolated all the time, especially with him stuck in that chair." Wayne was quiet for a moment as he considered what she had said. He knew that trauma could do a lot of things to people and maybe what both Timmy and Joyce needed were friends.

The party carried on for the rest of the afternoon, the kids played in the lake and even helped Timmy get in the water using floaties and a life jacket. The burn mark on his back and his legs drew a brief gasp at first but one of Danni's friend broke the tension, by showing of his scar from a four-wheeler accident. Joyce made her way around the grownups, chit chatting and flirting with the few unattached firefighters there, causing Kayla and Frankie to keep their distance and stay near Wayne. They hated badge bunnies and they had no desire to get to know her if that's what she was.

As the party wound down and people started to leave, Joyce found her way over to the trio of friends. "Thank you so much for having us," she said, smiling from ear to ear. "I don't know who had a better time, me or Timmy, it's been so tough since everything happened, ya know. We don't have many friends so all Timmy ever sees is me or his nurse, Malcolm."

Wayne nodded. "How are you holding up, Ms. Carson? I know that going through a fire can be very traumatic."

She nodded. "I wasn't there when it happened, it was a firefighter that rescued Timmy. I came home just as they pulled him out." She looked back at her son. "I think that's why he loves fire trucks so much." She looked down. "My husband was sleeping upstairs when it happened and he didn't get a chance to escape, they said."

She glanced away, Wayne assumed, to hide her tears but he couldn't be sure. "But honestly, you are the ones who experience it every day. I'm so thankful to people like you, people that saved my little Timmy."

Wayne smiled. "We just do our jobs, ma'am."

Frankie chimed in, "We wouldn't be good at anything else anyway."

Kayla scoffed, "You two wouldn't, I could be a model." They all shared a good laugh and any tension seemed to fade away. Joyce began asking about the firefighter life and the best and worst experiences they'd had. She seemed fascinated by some of their stories. As the night came to a close, she and Timmy were both sad to leave but Wayne said they would be invited to the next event because they enjoyed her company.

By the end of the night, Frankie and Wayne were left cleaning up the back yard. They had several trash bags full of bottles, cans and paper plates. Frankie checked to see if everyone had left then cleared his throat. "So when are you gonna leave bud?" he asked.

Wayne stood up, sighed and turned away. He'd been trying to avoid this conversation with everyone. "I haven't said yes yet bro, I'm not sure I'm gonna."

Frankie dropped his bag, clearly annoyed. "What the hell do you mean? This has been your dream for years. This was the fucking plan dude, make it to chief, you're almost there, why the fuck are you hesitating?"

Wayne didn't turn. He kept his voice calm and flat, "I'm not hesitating, I'm just not sure I'm ready to move on yet."

Frankie shook his head. "That's bullshit, you know it, the chief knows it and your dad knew it; so pull your head out of your ass."

Wayne spun on him, clearly in anger. "We don't know what my dad knew, do we? 'Cause he's not here; he was supposed to be here for it."

Frankie, not backing down, got right up in Wayne's face, "Did you do all this just for him, 'cause he told you not to do it?"

he roared. "Do you think if he was here, he'd want you to give up? This department was his baby — he took care of it and now you're really gonna let somebody else do it. Are you fucking serious?" The two stood facing each other, both clearly angry and both clearly hurt. Neither moved for a moment and anyone watching would almost be positive one of them was gonna swing.

Finally, Wayne took a deep breath and stepped back. Grabbing a beer, he sat and stared off into the distance. "See, this is why I'm glad you work for me, no one else would stand up to the captain like that," Frankie laughed.

"I don't fucking work for you." Grabbing his own beer and joining him, said, "I work for Scott, he works for you."

Wayne laughed. "I'm not ready for him to be gone, man."

"Yeah, but he wouldn't want you to let this chance pass you by."

Wayne took a swig. "Ya know, once I leave no one is gonna keep you and Kayla from killing each other."

Frankie smirked. "Come on, Scott will keep us straight."

"You must be crazy, Frankie, Scott will encourage you two to have a death match and sell tickets."

From the house, Crystal and Rea watched the exchange. Rea smiled, "Told you Frankie would get through to him."

Crystal nodded. "I know, I can't believe that worked, I've been avoiding having to deal with it for weeks now." She smiled really widely and squealed, "I'm gonna be a chief's wife."

Chapter 5

Wayne arrived at the next shift expecting things to be business as usual, only to find the chief and a member of the county council waiting for him. He hadn't said he was accepting the job and he wasn't aware of a meeting, so he was definitely curious about why they were there.

"Chief, Councilman Davis, to what do I owe the pleasure?" Both men seemed to have a genuine look of concern as if they were about to deliver horrible news.

The council man handed him a newspaper, folded open to the local   news section. The headline read:

'Serial Arsonist Plagues Local FD.'

Wayne looked twice to make sure he read it right, then looked at the two men, "Who went to the papers, I thought we were keeping the serial part under wraps?" They both looked at each other and then back at him. "Read the fourth paragraph, Wayne."

He scanned down and started reading: "This reporter has had the pleasure of spending time with these brave men and women and I can only hope that the culprit is brought to justice. The crew of Station 21 is a close family willing to put their lives on the line for each other and their community. However, it is possible an investigation is too much for local law enforcement and even with the leadership of men like Captain Miller, it can't be long before the worst could happen. The fact that it has taken police investigators three fires to begin investigations, shows the county's lack of concern for its responders."

Wayne scanned it again, then noticed the name of the reporter, Joyce Carson. She was a reporter and someone had told her everything about the current situation. "Son of a bitch," he said, slamming the paper down. "She's a fucking reporter."

The chief and councilman exchanged a glance, before saying together, "You know her!"

Wayne nodded. "So do you chief, she's that boy Timmy's mom, the one who survived that fire in Charlotte."

"That's who wrote this? Well, how did she find any of this out?" he asked.

Wayne paced around the room. "My wife invited her to Danni's birthday party yesterday, she was around the house for hours, anybody could've said something." He looked back at the paper. She hadn't bad-mouthed the department, just the police. Firefighters did that enough for fun anyway but now the arsonist knew that they knew and that could be very bad.

"Captain Miller," the councilman spoke, "I'm not going to place blame but this is a poor example for someone we are considering making assistant chief; I trust you will see to it information doesn't get out again. As a civil servant, it is important you put the best image forward for the county as a whole; after all this is an election year."

He had to bite his tongue. Politicians always pissed him off and he really didn't care about the elections anyway. After all, he usually voted for the other guy. He went to open his mouth and tell the councilman where to stick it when a loud tone rang throughout the building.

"Station 21, Engine 212, Ladder 21, Medic 9 respond — overturned vehicle with entrapment, intersection Highway 402 and Highway 52, Station 21, Engine 212, Ladder 21, Medic 9 respond — overturned vehicle with entrapment, intersection Highway 402 and Highway 52; time out 0923."

Wayne smirked. "Well, would you look at that? Saved by the bell. Chief, councilman if you'll excuse me." He grabbed his radio and started for the truck bay.

"We are not done discussing this Captain," the councilman called after him. Wayne laughed as he walked into the bay. As far as he was concerned, they could finish without him. He kicked off his shoes, stepped into his boots and pulled his bunker pants up before grabbing his coat and helmet and jumping in the captain's seat of Engine 212. No sooner than he put his head set on, he could hear Frankie's voice, "So, did they give you the badge already or was that just your first chance to kiss a councilman's ass."

Scott and Kayla both looked at him then Frankie, trying to suppress a giggle. "No, if anyone from this station is gonna kiss ass, I'll make sure it's you. Your wife told Crystal you're good at it." Laughter rolled through the interior of the truck as it pulled out of the bay, it's siren beginning to howl. "Dispatch this is Engine 212," Wayne said into the radio, "we're en route with five on board."

There was static followed by, "Copy Engine 212, multi vehicle MVA, one vehicle overturned with entrapment, unknown P.I.s."

"Copy dispatch, roll me a second medic, just in case."

"Copy Engine 212."

Another voice broke through the static. "Dispatch Ladder 21, Medic 9 en route," as the ladder truck and ambulance pulled out behind them. The three trucks sped along the highway, lights flashing and sirens blaring as they went. As they got closer to the accident, oncoming traffic was non-existent and traffic in front of them was backed up, forcing them to take the median down to the intersection.

At the scene were three vehicles: a black pick-up truck with damage to both the front and the rear, the second was a white sedan that had run partially under the pickup truck, the last vehicle was a green, small SUV, rolled over onto its roof. Glass was covering the street and two people seemed to be attempting to open the door to the overturned SUV, a third person was lying on the grass nearby, clutching his chest.

Captain Miller stepped down from the engine and surveyed the scene. A single deep breath was all he needed before he began giving orders.

"Scott take Watts and go check on the third vehicle, see what we got. Frankie you and Lee secure that SUV and get ready for extrication." He turned towards the ladder truck and its crew starting towards him. "Johnson, get me an inch and half charged and ready, Tillman and McMurray, I want you guys to sure up that truck. I don't want it moving until we get a tow here."

The team said nothing but went right to work. Wayne made his way over to the patient on the grass, already being worked on by the medics. "Mills, what do we have?" he asked. Mills was a young woman in her twenties with long, red hair and freckles. She had just become a paramedic but was very talented. She frowned, after an initial assessment and looked back at the captain. "He's got internal injuries Cap, looks like the airbag deployed but he wasn't wearing a seatbelt, contusions to the chest, abdomen distended and he's got a tib fib fracture. He's Cat Two but he's circling Cat One."

Wayne nodded. "Load and go," he said, turning towards the vehicles and speaking into his radio, "Dispatch, this is 21 command, Medic 9 is gonna be departing shortly with a possible

Cat One, what's the ETA on that second medic?" There was a pause and then a voice replied, "Command 21 showing Medic 10 is three minutes out." Wayne looked around and nodded, "Copy dispatch, still have two possible entrapments, go ahead and lift me a bird to the closest LZ." The voice replied, "Copy command, will advise when we have an ETA."

Wayne made his way to where Scott and Watts were with the driver of the white sedan. They had the door opened and Watts was in the back seat placing a collar on the driver's neck. She was a young woman, maybe still in High School. Scott was trying to dislodge her from underneath her steering column. "Captain, I think we might have to get a ram in here, she's pinned pretty good."

Wayne knelt and looked at the seat for a moment, before reaching between the young woman's feet, he pulled on the lever and began slowly pushing the seat back, freeing her pinned extremities. "Always check the seat, bud," he said, clapping Scott on the back. "Ma'am, Scott and Watts here are gonna take care of you until the medics arrive, okay?" The girl was clearly shaken but she managed a slight nod as they began bandaging what minor cuts she had.

By now, Tillman and McMurray had secured the truck in position with chocks, jacks and cribbing and joined Lee and Frankie on the SUV. Lee had broken out the back window and was crawling into the vehicle, Frankie was trying to get a response from the entrapped victim. Wayne knelt next to the vehicle. "Lee, what have we got?" he asked. He could hear him trying to pull down the back seat, followed by the simple words, "Oh fuck!" That was the sound of metal scraping and the whirr of a seat belt retracting. Lee was muttering on her way out, "Just breath baby, please just breath."

Wayne turned to Frankie. "Get that woman out asap!" and rushed to help Lee and she emerged holding a small child with a tuft of blonde hair. He didn't appear to be breathing and from the colour, he must have been upside down restrained by the car seat.

They rushed over to the side of the road and lay the small child down. Wayne grabbed a small mask from the medical kit and placed it over the child's mouth, using it to squeeze air into its lungs. Lee checked for a pulse, then pulled out the AED and began placing the pads on the child's chest while Wayne started CPR.

The machine gave off a shrill sound before saying, "Shock advised, shocked advised, stand clear." Wayne stopped CPR and moved back slightly, Lee pressed the button, there was a loud sound and the child's body jumped, then a pause. The machine said, "Continue CPR," and Wayne double-checked for a pulse and went back to compressing the young boy's chest. After a minute, the machine again said, "Shock advised, shock advised, stand clear." Wayne backed up and looked at Lee, she pressed the button and again the child's body jumped. Time seemed to move excruciatingly slowly as they waited; a few seconds were an eternity. Then the child gasped and coughed. Lee grabbed the oxygen and put it on the child. "I got him Cap, go help the others."

As he made his way back to the vehicle, Medic 10 arrived and the sound of a helicopter could be heard approaching. The crew had stabilised the car and pulled off one side of doors so they could access the mother. She was breathing but had an obvious head injury. It took all four of them to lower her gently down and properly onto a backboard. A third medic had self-responded to the scene and they were already loading the patient from the other vehicle when Medic 10 arrived. One medic went to check on the child who Lee was caring for while the other, Lemar, came to where they were, freeing the patient from the car.

Once the extrication was complete, Frankie drove them to the landing zone while Lee rode in the back, helping take care of the child. Wayne supervised the clean-up as tow trucks arrived and picked up the smashed vehicles. Medic 9 passed by on their way back to the station before the scene was fully cleared and traffic restored to normal. With all the carnage and destruction, there was still no loss of life when Engine 212 finally cleared the scene and made its way back to the station. It was a good day so far; then again, it wasn't even time for lunch yet.

Chapter 6

As the day drew on Station 21 ran call after call. Just after lunch, they responded to a man who fell from a roof he was working on. There was a kitchen fire caused by a young girl trying to make grilled cheese. While they were making dinner, there was another car accident which pushed their meal back to much later in the evening.

It was after ten at night and Captain Miller was still working on paperwork when the last truck pulled back in from a small woods fire near the train tracks. He was expecting Watts to walk in with the report so he didn't look up, when someone came into the office and just stood there.

"Put it over on the pile Watts, I'm almost finished with the last accident report."

A feminine voice responded, "Ummm Captain Miller, I don't think I'm Watts."

He looked up to see Joyce Carson, dressed in a tight-fitting top and mid-length skirt. She gave him a weak smile and waved like a cartoon character who knew they were in trouble. "I came by earlier but you were out on calls. I wanted to talk to you if you had a minute."

Wayne scowled and looked back at his paperwork. "I don't give statements to the press, Mrs Carson, that's the Battalion Chief you need to talk to."

She stepped back slightly and nodded. "They said you were upset but I didn't think you'd be rude, captain."

He looked up at her, clearly annoyed. "You didn't tell any of us you were a reporter, you gave out information the department didn't want revealed. I'm not being rude, I'm being smart."

"I'm really sorry. I should've said something but it never came up and I didn't mean to cause problems for the department. I honestly think the world of all of you and I thought that the public needed to know what you were up against." She crossed her arms and leaned back a little, looking across the table at him.

Wayne could feel the headache starting already as he began to rub the bridge of his nose. He could believe she had good intentions but he couldn't believe that she didn't know that revealing that information wouldn't cause trouble. Maybe she was trying to save as much face as possible, maybe she was trying to give him an excuse next time he talked to the councilman. Either way, he figured he'd hear her out. Maybe having a reporter on the department's side wouldn't be a bad idea and maybe getting struck by lightning felt great.

"Okay," he said, motioning her towards a chair, "have a seat. Tell me what's on your mind." She clapped in glee and bounced before sitting in the seat.

"I want to do a series on firefighters and their day-to-day life. I want to show the community what kind of heroes you all really are. You've done so much for Timmy and I feel like this could give a little back."

Yep, he had a headache now. It wasn't a bad idea but without the council signing off on it, there would be hell to pay. Especially because it would look like the fire department was encouraging her words about the police department.

"Look Mrs. Carson," he said, trying to not sound as annoyed as he did, "I like the idea but it would have to be approved through the council and the chief and then there would be paperwork."

She smiled. "I don't wanna do this as a reporter captain. I want to be a volunteer to really get a feel for the department."

Wayne was speechless. The department was once a one hundred percent   volunteer department throughout the county. When it became a single unified department, that changed to about twenty-five per cent. Almost all volunteers were auxiliary personnel with minimum training. They normally assisted on large calls, or handled things at the station that the paid members didn't get to during their shift while running calls. They trained with the firefighters and responded and sometimes a couple would stay overnight to help the shift. They all had full-time jobs and families and did this as a way to help the community. Joyce seemed to want to do this to help her career.

"Joyce being a volunteer is serious and not a way to help your career," he said flatly. "I'm not telling you that you can't do it; we never turn volunteers away unless they have a criminal record. But if it's not serious to you, it's not fair to the other volunteers."

Joyce smiled and nodded in agreement. "Oh, I know how serious this is and I'm willing to put in the work, captain. I just want to be able to give back after how kind you've all been to me and my son." She paused for a moment, "Please Wayne?"

Wayne begrudgingly reached into his desk and pulled out a volunteer application. He handed it to her. "Fill this out and take it to headquarters in town, they'll assign you to us after your background check." Joyce grinned wide and started to say something but the high pitch tones cut the conversation short.

"Station 21, Station 5, Station 7, Battalion 2, Medic 1 respond — structure fire 415 West Street: Avery Propane Industries, Station 21, Station 5, Station 7, Battalion 2, Medic 1 respond — structure fire 415 West Street Avery Propane Industries," The radio announced. Wayne went pale. Avery Propane was the office for the local propane distributor. While the building only housed offices and meeting rooms, behind the building was a tanker yard which held thousands of gallons of the highly flammable material in several different sized pressurised containers. If this was already involved, he knew he could use the Battalion Chief to start staging units here, to support on scene efforts but he'd still need additional medic units and Hazardous Materials teams.

He ran from the office, not even saying goodbye to his guest and quickly donned his gear. The others were already in the truck. Grabbing the radio he spoke hastily, "Dispatch Station 21, Engine 212, Engine 210 and Ladder 21 responding Avery Propane Industries, drop additional tones for Haz-Mat and have law enforcement en route for traffic control." He knew getting law enforcement on route early would help with keeping onlookers at bay.

"Copy Engine 212," the radio replied, followed by a second voice, "Dispatch Ladder 7, Engine 71, Squad 76 en route to Avery Propane," and then a third, "Dispatch show Engine 51, Engine 52 and Battalion 2 en route."

Sirens called out into the night as the three trucks from Station 21 raced towards the scene. Avery Propane was only about two miles from the station and when they arrived, flames were coming out the front of the building obscuring the view of the storage yard out the back. The building wasn't more than a thousand square feet and only one storey, with metal sidings and large, glass windows on the front. The few workers who had been present when it started were already outside, staring back at the inferno as Engine 212 took its position.

Wayne didn't have to tell his crew anything at first as they began pulling a hose from the truck and playing it out so that it would be ready to fill. Engine 210 hooked a hydrant on its way in and was laying a five-inch line in with it. As soon as they parked, they hooked up to Engine 212 and began to supply water.

Wayne quickly checked the back of the building to see if the fire had spread towards the tanker yard, then ran back to the trucks. "Watts, grab McMurray and get a water cannon set up on the rear of the building. I want a wall of water between the building and that yard," he called out to the two firefighters waiting by Engine 210. Frankie and Lee had already masked up and were waiting for the go ahead to enter with a line charged at the door. Wayne could see flames were breaching the roof so the building should have been ventilated, he gave the signal and Frankie took out the glass of the front door with a Halligan Bar.

Frankie grabbed the nozzle of the hose and Lee leaned into his back as he opened it, spraying water into the entryway, knocking back the flames which greeted them on the inside of the building. The hiss of their air packs was the only sound they could hear as they made their way into the building. The flames coming from a room off to the left, seemed to indicate that would be where the seat of the fire was. Slowly, they crawled their way to the door and saw a room completely engulfed in flame.

Once again, Frankie opened the nozzle spraying a wide fog into the air, before narrowing his stream and working from the ceiling down the walls. The glass on the windows had already blackened and when the water hit it, the window shattered. The quick introduction of fresh air caused the flames to burn hotter but Frankie and Lee held fast and continued their attack. Gradually the fire was knocked down though the damage to this corner of the building was extensive.

Water was raining down from above Frankie and Lee through the absent roof as they began hitting hot spots. A second team from Station 7 had entered the building and was beginning an overhaul: the process to check for fire spread using hand tools. They made their way through to another room closer to the back of the building. As they poked and prodded the ceiling, other firefighters outside placed fans to blow fresh air into the building and clear out the smoke.

An unlucky hit and a charred area of the ceiling dropped down — a single piece of flaming debris falling onto some cloth sitting in the corner. The cloth quickly ignited and seconds later, something underneath exploded out, showering the room and the two firefighters with flaming liquid. Frankie heard the noise from the other room and opened his nozzle in a full fog, as he proceeded to douse both men and the room, beating back the flames. He screamed out for anyone that could hear him as he tried to rescue his fallen brothers.

It was only seconds for additional teams to rush into the building but for Frankie and Lee it seemed like an eternity. They doused the entire room leaving a strange device where the cloth had been, partially burned but intact enough to explain the cause of the second flame up. As the other crews rescued the downed firefighters, Frankie and Lee began to search for anything else that looked remotely suspicious, before backing out of the building themselves.

**

Wayne and Scott were directing the salvage operations outside when they heard what sounded like a small explosion followed by Frankie screaming from inside the building. They grabbed their masks and threw them, as firefighters from Station 5 began to head to the back of the building. It took them seconds to find Frankie, spraying water, desperately trying to knock down flames in an otherwise unburnt room. On the floor were the men from station 7, one of them clutching his face and writhing in pain the other still patting down his coat and pants. Wayne and Scott grabbed the first man and quickly carried him out to the medics waiting outside, it was clear he'd suffered burns to the left-side of his face. A minute later, the second firefighter was carried out by his rescuers from Station 5.

Wayne ripped off his own mask and grabbed the man. "What happened in there?" The other firefighters were trying to put an oxygen mask on him but he pushed it away momentarily. "We were doing overhaul when something in that room exploded on us, captain." He then grabbed the mask and began taking deep breaths.

Wayne looked back at the firefighter being loaded into the ambulance, then at Frankie and Lee as they emerged from the building. Their eyes met and a sense of realisation hit them all at the same time; the arsonist had struck again. This time hospitalising one of their own.

Chapter 7

A relief crew had come in to man the station almost immediately after the accident. When Engine 212 rolled back into the station, Barry, the department's Battalion Chief, was waiting for them with a department chaplain to offer counselling to anyone after the incident. Barry was up there in years and it showed in the lines on his face and the padding around his waist. His hair was snow white and sometime ago he'd decided that he deserved to have a beard, making him look even more like a mall Santa when he wore his glasses. He made his way across the bay to the truck and waited for Wayne to step out.

Barry gave him a concerned look then glanced back at the chaplain. "Wayne, I think your team needs to debrief, especially if you're gonna go to the hospital." Wayne looked over at the chaplain, who nervously tried not to make eye contact.

"Did you bring the guy I laid out that time dad almost died?" he asked. Barry tried his best not to laugh but a small giggle made its way out.

"Is that him? You sure? My memory ain't what it used to be," he said, giving Wayne a warning glance.

Wayne began removing his gear and arranging his uniform. "He can check with the others; you know me and God don't talk about problems." He turned to walk towards the door and paused, turning back, "He should probably stay away from Casselman, he hits harder than I do."

Wayne used the shocked expression on his face to make and

escape from the talk Barry no doubt wanted to have. He was angry, he wanted to yell and beat the shit out of something. He wanted to focus his anger at something and unleash. He couldn't do that though, because he had no clue who to blame other than himself. He made his way to his office to grab a few things and then out the door he went.

Barry was waiting for him outside; for an old guy he was fast as hell. Wayne sighed, realising Barry wasn't gonna give up until they had a talk. He resigned that the conversation could take place if they went to the hospital together, so he turned and jumped in the passenger seat of the Battalion Chief's response truck. "Fine, we'll do this but you're driving old man."

For the first few minutes they both were silent. Wayne wasn't sure what pissed him off more, the fact that Barry wouldn't let him go alone or the fact that he wasn't getting this over with. Since he was a teenager, Barry had always stepped in with some sage advice from the days of yore, it was his thing. His advice always came from a good place but to Wayne, tonight wasn't the night.

When he decided he'd had enough, Wayne broke the silence. "I know you're gonna tell me to calm down, it's not my fault but what the fuck do you expect me to do?" He crossed his arms and stared out the window.

Barry gave a sigh. "Well, if you know that, maybe I should say something else." He paused briefly. "Did your dad ever tell you about Jerome Watson?" The confused look on Wayne's face was his answer. "I didn't think he ever did; he didn't like talking about it. It was really early on, back when it was just a collection of volunteer departments. I was working for EMS at the time and it was late one night after a rough storm. See, Jerome lived down the road from the power plant and had this old souped up '67

Camaro. He'd run the roads in that thing like he was on the track. Your daddy always told that boy he was gonna kill someone doing that. But Jerome was young and didn't listen to nobody."

Wayne began to wonder if this story was going anywhere as Barry continued, "So that night your dad, Chief Rose and me and my partner were all at Paddy Hutt getting a bite. It was just after 10:00 p.m. and we had just been through this rough thunderstorm when we got the call. Motor vehicle accident with entrapment and one vehicle on fire. Chief Rose took off for the station while your old man followed us to the scene." Barry took a breath and shook his head a little. "It was a bad scene, just terrible. Jerome must've been doing about ninety when he hit the couple in the truck head on. He came to a stop about twenty feet off the roadway into the woods, the truck got knocked on its side and slid back about fifty feet. As near as we could tell, the young woman died right there on impact, broke her neck going out the passenger side window. The husband crawled out the truck with both his legs broken. Me and my partner ran to him, your dad went for Jerome. He was still screaming as the car burned and your dad couldn't do a damn thing. He couldn't even get near the car to help him."

"It must've been about three minutes 'til a truck got on scene with us and your dad kept everyone back. He took the line himself, while Chief Rose ran the truck and he put the fire out and made the call for the coroner. I had to go check the body, what was left of it, to confirm it was a D.O.A. and I gotta say it still gives me nightmares. I can only imagine what he went through."

Barry turned into the hospital parking lot and quickly found a space to park. Once he put the truck in park, he looked Wayne in his eyes. "That night would have broken your father, he could've easily blamed himself, even though none of it was his fault. But it didn't, he learned more from that night than I'd reckon he learned in any class. After that he went out and bought a foam and a dry chem extinguisher to keep on his personal truck. He encouraged having a program where we kept one man in the station at all times, just to make sure a truck rolled. He carried Jerome with him, not as a burden but as inspiration, inspiration to be better."

Wayne had heard so many of his father's stories but never this one. He was both shocked and proud of the man who raised him. The fact that something so horrible never stopped him from wanting to help people, reminded him why William Miller was so loved by the department. "Barry, he never told me any of that." he said, the shock still very evident on his face.

Barry gave a chuckle. "He never spoke about it except to me and the chief and usually when he was driving a point. He became adamant about change, about improving not just his department but the whole county. He started the movement to unify the stations under one chief, even helped to interview potential chiefs."

"When he settled on Jimmy Frances and we agreed, the first thing Jimmy did was hire Chief Rose as his assistant and me and your father as Battalion Chiefs. Your dad was a man who just wanted to help people but you know that. What you didn't know is he was angry so many times and every time, we'd go for a drive and he'd tell me he had to forget his anger, because being angry wasn't gonna fix the problem. So son, forget your damn anger because being angry won't fix that boy in there."

Barry got out of the truck and left Wayne sitting there for a moment to think about what he said. Wayne had been furious but what good did it do? He had people relying on him and being angry wouldn't help. He always remembered his dad saying, "It never mattered how mad you got, the crops wouldn't come in 'til you went and got em." It made a lot more sense now.

Wayne got out of the truck and caught up with Barry. They made their way into the hospital and went straight towards the emergency department. Wayne wasn't angry any more; he knew being mad wouldn't help. He was determined, determined to see his friend was okay and get back on shift as soon as possible. Determined to make sure he did everything he could, to keep this from happening again.

Chapter 8

As Barry and Wayne made their way into the waiting room, they were greeted with a gathering of solemn faces in differing stages of gear. Some obviously from the truck crew of the two victims were still in full turnout, only missing their helmets and masks. Still, others in the assembly were in full or partial uniform. Ted the captain from station 5, quickly made his way over to the new arrivals.

"Barry, Wayne," he said, "we don't have any news yet on Sammy but it looks like Greg only suffered minor burns." He glanced back over his shoulder at a young woman sitting nearest to the registration desk. "That's Sammy's wife, Sarah, if you wanted to go and talk to her."

Barry gave Wayne a nod, signalling him to go over. As Wayne approached, the young woman glanced up, her make-up clearly smeared with tears. "Chief Miller," she said, "thank you so much for coming."

"It's still captain ma'am," Wayne corrected her, making a mental note that the news of his yet-secured promotion was getting way out of hand. "If there's anything we can do, let me know; Station 21 is here for you and your family."

She tried to work up a smile but it clearly wasn't in her, "Thank you, I just wish I knew what happened, he's always so careful." She looked back over her shoulder at the door leading back to where the operating rooms were.

Wayne's face tightened but he forced himself not to growl

his response. Still, it came out cold and angry. "That's exactly what I intend to find out, ma'am."

He gave her a nod and made his way to where Ted and Barry were standing talking with Bobby, the station 7 captain. Wayne and Bobby had come up together at the Academy. They had always carried on in friendly competition with one another, each one pushing the other to be better. Normally, they greeted each other with a small jibe about the other failing at something but today, Wayne just grabbed his counterpart and hugged him.

Bobby returned the hug briefly then placed a hand on his shoulder. "You got him out of there Wayne, thank you."

Wayne nodded. "I didn't do anything special; my team got the flames out and the medics got him here."

"What the hell happened, man? I thought we had it out, I mean we were on overhaul."

Wayne glanced at Barry and Ted. "I heard an explosion, not very big, before Casselman started screaming. I'm not sure what it was but David should be there now trying to figure it out."

Ted gnashed his teeth together. "Tell me you don't think it's that son of bitch that almost got us at Jefferies."

Wayne had forgotten Ted had a habit of going into the buildings, even though he was a captain. He hadn't realised he may have been inside before the collapse 'til now. "That's exactly what I think; it's the only thing that makes sense."

Bobby's face went slack and Wayne knew what was going through his head before he said it. "Are we being targeted, Wayne?"

Barry chimed in before he could answer, "There's no way of knowing anything like that, so let's not jump to conclusions." He looked around the room at the assembled group of firefighters and family. "There's no point in spreading something like that."

Wayne shook his head. "Doesn't matter either way; we do our job. We watch each other's backs and when we find this bastard, we make sure he gets nailed to the wall,"

The three other officers all grunted and nodded in agreement. As they did, a nurse wheeled out the first of the two injured firefighters. His left arm was bandaged and he was clearly still feeling whatever painkiller they had given him. Bobby was the first one to get to him and make sure he was okay.

"You all right Greg?" he asked, taking the chair from the nurse. "What did the doctors say?"

Greg smiled. "I'm good, Cap, they said I only got a couple of second degree burns on my arm and shoulder. Where's Sammy?"

Bobby looked back at the door to the ER. "The doctors haven't come out with an update yet but he's in good hands." He looked back at Greg trying to give him a reassuring smile.

"It was my fault, Cap," Greg said, almost tearing up. "I was poking the ceiling before we checked the whole room."

"Bullshit," Wayne said from across the room, where he had been leaning on the wall. He stood up and walked over to Greg. "That's total bullshit, son. You were doing a standard overhaul, like you were trained." He leaned down and looked Greg in the eye. "You did a fine job in there and what happened to Sammy was not your fault."

The room was quiet and everyone stared at Wayne for a moment, as he locked eyes with the young firefighter. Greg's face tightened and he nodded his understanding of the senior officer's words.

Wayne stood back up and looked around the room raising his voice for the entire room to hear, "This is the job. We can do it right every single day and it can still get us. We can't blame ourselves when things we can't control go sideways. The only thing we can do is learn from situations like this and support one another. So, don't carry this like a weight on your shoulders, use it like fuel to drive you to be better every day. Be better for yourselves. Be better for each other, the men and women standing right next to you. 'Cause when the next tone drops, we don't have time for doubts; doubts cause accidents. We have to be ready and willing to go as far as we need to and get the job done."

There was a brief moment of shocked silence, followed by an uproar of cheers and agreement. Wayne looked back at Barry who nodded in approval and thought about what his dad had always told him: '*it never mattered how angry you got, the crops won't come in 'til you go out and get em*'. It made sense to him now. After all these years he was still learning from his old man. That thought brought a slight smile to his face.

Bobby leaned over to him and quietly chided, "Now you wanna start acting like a chief?"

Wayne looked over his shoulder and quipped back, "Watch or I'll tell them to give you the damn job."

Bobby threw his hands up and backed away, chuckling. "Nope, I am not getting stuck in an office."

For a moment the mood was lighter, they were still hurt and angry but they knew they had each other. Suddenly, the doors to the OR opened and a doctor walked out, his mask still around his neck. The room went silent as Bobby and Sarah walked over to him. There was a hushed conversation followed by Sarah covering her mouth and sobbing. Bobby hugged her and then let her go with the doctor as he came back to the rest of the assembled group.

Bobby cleared his throat. "Sammy is stable, they've done all they can for now. He's in a medically-induced coma, will be for a couple of days. He has third degree burns to his face and neck and second degree to his arms and torso. If your team hadn't got him out when you did, he might not have made it."

The room was silent, they avoided the worst but they all knew a burn like that was hard to come back from. It was a punch in the gut and they all felt it. For a moment, the strength they all had shared was sapped away.

Bobby walked over to Wayne and clapped him on the shoulder, his eyes tearing up. "We're gonna keep being better for Sammy, brother, we're gonna keep being better for him."

Chapter 9

Frankie didn't go to the hospital. He knew there was nothing he could do and he wasn't in the mood to sit around and wonder about what ifs. He made a quick call home to check-in and calm down his already worried wife. Then he got in his car and drove back to the scene of the fire.

He parked next to the Fire Marshal's truck and slid on his boots, pants and helmet before making his way into the building. Sylvia was gathering several small bags and locking them in a toolbox before placing an evidence tag. She nodded to him and continued on with her work. David was next to the wall examining something, clearly fascinated by what he had found.

Frankie walked into the second room where the devices had exploded. There was minor damage from the flaming liquid but they had extinguished it before it could do significant damage. He stared at the corner where the device had been. The carpet had been cut away and a small portion of the wall was cut open, apparently the item Sylvia had collected. The room was probably used for lunch breaks and meetings during the day.

Frankie walked through the opposite door which seemed to me a type of locked room. He noted that the wall adjoining this and the previous room was a significant fire wall and would have taken some time for fire to spread into this room. This was obviously because this room led out into the storage yard behind the building. The fire wall probably ran the length of the building to protect the propane storage, in case the building caught fire.

He couldn't help but wonder if the arsonist knew this when he set up his devices, or was it just dumb luck he set them in the front of the building and behind that wall. He continued roaming the building when a gruff voice behind drew him from his thoughts.

"You weren't supposed to be here," David said, standing behind him.

Frankie turned and nodded. "I'm sorry man, I just wanted to see if I could help."

David shook his head. "No, I mean the arsonist didn't plan on anybody being here when this went off, I think."

Frankie was confused. "What do you mean? The fire started with employees in the building, not really following you there, bud."

David held up a bag which held a clearly melted surge protector. "This is what started the fire, it was overloaded in that first office, the arsonist's device wasn't supposed to go off 'til later."

Frankie took the bag and looked at the charred and melted plastic. "You sure this was the cause, not a different device or some chemical concoction."

David nodded. "Oh, I'm sure. In fact, last time this building was inspected this power strip was actually noted and they were told to fix it before it caused a fire." He looked around for a second. "I'm gonna do a thorough check to see what else I had previously cited them for, that they may have ignored."

Frankie punched the wall next to him, then cussed because his knuckles hurt. "So, dumb luck and stupid employees are why we got a firefighter sitting in the hospital right now, is that what you're telling me?"

David shook his head again. "No, he's in that hospital

because someone wanted to cause damage, he just wasn't the target. You know damn well you can't control fire like this guy tries to."

Frankie remembered the old scene from the movie Backdraft where De Niro described fire as an animal; he wasn't far off in his description. Fire can be steered and controlled but it will always try to do what it wants. The arsonist was definitely trying to master fire but everyone who ever went up against the beast knew, fire has no master.

David could see the wheels turning in Frankie's head. "Look, there is a silver lining here. We have the device and that's thanks to your quick action."

Frankie shrugged. "I just keep trying to figure out if I did everything I could. I keep replaying it in my head, David."

David placed a hand on his shoulder. "Take a lesson from an old timer, don't. You didn't do this man, fire did and you put that beast down, just like you're supposed to."

Frankie nodded. "I guess you may be right, it's just hard to not think about it." David gave a small smile.

"I know, believe me but you gotta remember that all we can do is our best and you did that. Now, get outta here, there's nothing left here for now."

***

When Frankie arrived home, he was surprised to see April Wells sitting on his porch with his wife. There was a time when it would be commonplace for her to be around, they served in the corps together after all and were great friends in High School. It wasn't until she put on the badge that things became a little awkward.

It was stupid really but it's universally known that

firefighters and police officers just don't mesh well. It's kind of like cats and dogs, they can live together in harmony but eventually, one is gonna piss the other one off just on general principle. The friendship April Wayne and Frankie had enjoyed since High School had suffered that same principle.

April, however, was counting on a stronger bond she shared with Frankie that would trump all of the other mess. As he walked up the steps with a sour look on his face, she stood. Her hands on her hips, she gave a smile and greeted him.

"Oorah, Marine," she said, as he stepped on to the porch.

Frankie tilted his head for a moment then returned the smile and offered a fist bump, "Oorah!"

April bumped his fist then chuckled. "Glad to see some things don't change."

Frankie nodded. "Nope, some things last forever. What's on your mind?"

April sat down in one of the handmade chairs on his porch and handed him a thick file. "That's everything I've got on the fires so far, not a lot of physical evidence on the first three," she said, as he leafed through the pages.

"Looks like the only physical evidence was melted plastic and an alcohol-based accelerant."

"Exactly," she nodded, "which is why we interviewed the guys at the station first, because?"

"Whoever did this, knew enough to use a difficult to trace, easily accessible chemical and components that would burn quickly." He answered, realising that the arsonist was more dangerous than they had first thought.

"So, at first it looked like random buildings but look at the company that holds both the insurance and contract on those three properties."

Frankie glossed over it at first but now he saw the same name repeatedly. "Fishburn Property Management Corp, who are they?"

April smiled. "I'm glad you asked young padawan, they are a subsidiary of Nash development, a company that has been constructing a lot of major developments in the area."

Frankie scratched his head. "Nash, why is that name familiar?" He knew he'd heard it recently.

April handed him a political pamphlet and on the front was the same councilman who had been yelling at the captain. The name in big red letters was Coleman Nash. Frankie was shocked for a moment, then his shock turned to anger. "You think this is the asshole trying to burn us?"

April shrugged. "I don't know if it's him but I figure he's connected. Now, if I told Wayne and he went in there half-cocked and said the wrong thing, there goes his career but if me and you go nosing around, well …"

Frankie nodded. "We go kick up the brush, see what snakes rattle out, I got you. I'm in."

April smiled. "Well, hurry up and get changed, I wanna catch him at the office and throw him off his game, ya know just in case."

Frankie quickly changed, throwing on some khaki pants and a nice polo shirt before grabbing his old .38 special and jumping in the car with April. She opened her glove box and gave him a knowing look, so Frankie could store his weapon there. Frankie turned on the radio and synced his phone to it. The song he chose began with the sound of three loud church bells followed by the energetic opening of Metallica, 'For Whom the Bell Tolls'.

***

It was mid-afternoon when they pulled in front of the three-storey building that acted as the offices for the Lake County Government. The building was constructed in the mid-nineties to house all of the county offices under one roof. On the first storey there was the county council chambers and the county treasury office. The third floor was reserved for emergency services, including the dispatch centre and the county emergency operations centre. Frankie and April were heading to the second floor which housed the offices for most of the county administration.

When they stepped out of the elevator, a detective was waiting, leaning against the wall holding a manilla envelope in his hand. He was an older gentleman but clearly fit, his caramel-coloured skin showing very few lines. He smiled when he saw them and walked over towards April and Frankie and handed them the envelope.

April smiled. "Frankie, this Captain Cline, he's over the detective division and also handles our reserved officer training."

Frankie nodded. "Pleased to meet you captain, you guys already have a warrant? I didn't think there was any hard evidence."

April opened the envelope, pulled out the papers and handed them to Frankie. "Oh, we don't have a warrant yet, these are the papers to make you a reserve officer, that way you're covered to work this with me. Congrats I'm your FTO."

Captain Cline slid his sleeve up, revealing a tattoo of the Eagle Globe and Anchor. "You know what they say Officer Carson, once a Marine …"

Frankie signed the papers and handed them to him before finishing his sentence, "Always a marine, Oorah."

The captain handed him a badge which Frankie quickly slid on his belt and then they made their way to Councilman Nash's office. The Councilman was packing up to leave as they walked in. He looked up, seeing them and began questioning their presence.

"Can I help you officers? Are you perhaps lost?" he sneered, with an oily air of confidence.

The captain smiled and his voice became velvet smooth. "Why not at all, sir, we're doing this investigation and we just need to ask some questions about Nash Developments. It's your family's firm, correct?"

The councilman seemed to be offended by the question. "It's run by my brother in Charlotte but I really don't have anything to do with the company other than being a shareholder."

April decided to press forward and hopefully force a stumble in the sleazy politician. "Yes sir, we're aware. Are you also familiar with Fishburn Property Management Corp?"

If the councilman was at all phased by the question, he didn't show it and answered quite calmly, "Yes ma'am, it's a company I helped my brother procure a couple of years ago. It has properties here, in Myrtle Beach and Charleston, basically all over the state."

April and the captain looked at one another, then back to Councilman Nash. "Who would gain if a property owned by the company was destroyed?"

The councilman sat down. "If one of the Fishburn properties here were destroyed that would be terrible. It could cost the company hundreds of thousands of dollars; the deal wasn't gonna turn profit for some time."

None of them expected that answer, nor did they expect to see the councilman genuinely concerned about the possibility of the company going under. April and Frankie exchanged a glance then she spoke, "Mr Nash, so far four buildings owned and insured by Fishburn have been burned. Can you think of why that would be happening?"

The councilman went white. Clearly, he was more connected to this then he was letting on but, he didn't know all four buildings were his brother's company's property. "I knew about the deal for the Old Jefferies building but I didn't know what other properties they owned. I couldn't possibly have known; I wasn't privy to that information. My brother funds almost half of my re-election campaign, if his company went under that would be horrible."

Frankie slammed his hand onto the desk causing the councilman to jump. "Last night, a firefighter got his face burned off by whoever's doing this and a building came down on me. Are you honestly gonna look at me and tell me that your re-election being in danger is horrible?"

The councilman began to read the room, his face contorting slightly with the realisation of how actionable a position he was in. "Please, I had no idea. I will make some calls to get you any information you need, just please, don't connect this to me." The pure fear on the face of a man who had tried to bully his captain twenty-four hours earlier brought, a menacing grin to Frankie's face. April stepped up, her tone matter of fact as she handed him a card.

"My fax number is on there. Have them send me everything relevant to properties and contracts that they have in the area. As long as we get credible information, we'll make sure the report shows how you cooperated with the investigation."

She didn't wait for a reply, just turned dismissively and walked out of his office followed by Frankie and Captain Cline.

They were quiet until they entered the elevator, walking with the intention of looking menacing. Once the elevator doors closed Frankie spoke up.

"That was a waste of time, he didn't even know they owned all four properties."

Captain Cline shook his head. "No, he didn't but he damn sure knew how it made him look being connected."

April nodded. "Exactly, so whoever is doing this either has a problem with Nash or with his brother's company."

"So, where do we go next, Detective, Fishburn?" Frankie asked.

April and Cline nodded in unison as the elevator doors opened and they made their way out of the building. Their next stop would be Fishburn Property Management Corp.

Chapter 10

Fishburn Property Management Corp had a small office building not too far from the county offices. When April and Frankie pulled up, they found security appearing to tussle with a woman in front of the building. They exchanged a glance and pulled up alongside the front door only to see Joyce Carson struggling to free her arm from a mountain of a security guard.

"Get your hands off me, you mongoloid!" she screamed, "I'm not going away, they are going to answer for what they did, damn it."

The guard shoved her away, causing her to fall. "Just get outta here lady, or next time my bosses might not be so nice."

April walked up, holding her badge. "Mind explaining what you mean by that, sir?" as Frankie helped Joyce up from the ground.

"She's been coming here yelling and screaming for weeks, next time we might just press charges is all," the guard replied, stepping back with his hands visible so he didn't appear to be a threat.

Frankie stepped up. "Well, since we're here, why don't we have a talk with your employer? He would be ..."

The guard turned pale for a second, not sure what to say. "Well, Mr Fishburn runs this office, so he would be in charge but as I told the lady, he's not in today and he's specifically requested she not be allowed on the premises any more."

Frankie and April exchanged a glance before asking

simultaneously, "Any more?"

Joyce glared defiantly at the guard. "You tell him, his company will answer for what they've done. I will see him and his six chins in court."

April pulled her away, leaving Frankie with the guard. The guard regarded him and clearly would've preferred the other of the two. Frankie grinned at him and enjoyed that he made this man uncomfortable. "So, tell me why Mr. Fishburn isn't in the office today, Chuckles?"

'Chuckles' seemed to put him off his guard even more causing him to stammer his response. "Mr. Fishburn had to fly to Charlotte a couple days ago for an emergency meeting with the new owners. I can't really say why, b-b-b-but he seemed pretty upset."

Frankie scowled. If he was in Charlotte, there was no way he targeted the propane facility. He looked back at Chuckles. "Who's in the office now that would be in charge   ?"

The guard paused. "Ms. Reyes, his assistant is still here and a few of the other office workers."

The thought of a new suspect made Frankie smile. "Perfect, go tell Ms. Reyes we want to have a talk to her and we'll be right in, after we decide if this young lady needs to press charges." He had no idea if she actually could but he figured it would light a fire under Chuckles' ass. Frankie turned and joined April and Joyce. He really wanted to know what the reporter, who blabbed about the arsonist in the first place, was doing here.

"Thank you so much, it's good to see you again Frankie," she said, straightening her clothing.

April raised an eyebrow, looking at the two of them. "You two know each other?"

From her look, Frankie could tell April had the wrong idea.

"April this is Joyce Carson, the reporter, her son loves coming to the station and seeing the fire trucks."

April's eyes widened. "Oh, so you're that reporter, really?"

Joyce crossed her arms. "What do you mean that reporter? And Frankie, why are you here with the police?"

April and Frankie exchanged a curious glance. "I'm just doing a ride along to get my mind off things but then we found you. What's going on here?"

Joyce apparently bought his line, as she scoffed and motioned towards the office building. "This is the local office of the developers that are refusing to take responsibility for the faulty electrical work they used." She turned towards the building screaming, "THAT BURNED MY SON AND KILLED MY HUSBAND!"

April made a mental note to revisit that discussion. "But surely it wasn't this office that constructed your house in Charlotte, was it?"

Joyce shook her head and pulled a piece of paper from her purse. "No but this is where the latest settlement letter came from. Look at this, it's a joke!"

April took the paper from her. It was a letter from this exact office and signed by one Raymond Fishburn. The letter stated that, some responsibility may be held by Nash Developments and its subsidiaries as insurers of the property. It also stated they were not primarily responsible for any medical issues or deaths as a result of the fire. It offered Joyce a settlement of three hundred thousand dollars for the loss of her home and possessions.

She handed the letter to Frankie. "What do you make of this?" glancing back at the office doors.

Frankie read over the letter. "Wait these guys are denying fault. Didn't you say that the fire started because they knowingly use faulty electrical parts?"

Joyce nodded. "Exactly, I have records and memos proving they knew and the reports all state the fire started from an outlet that malfunctioned in the master bedroom."

April put on the best smile she could. "Joyce, do you think we could look at those reports? Maybe we can help you and find something they missed."

Joyce nodded her head. "I have it all at home, you're welcome to come by and look at it. I can even make copies."

"That's great Joyce," Frankie said slowly, leading her away from the building to her minivan. "We're gonna have a talk with whoever is in charge here and then we'll come by and get it."

Joyce beamed. "You really are just wonderful, Frankie. I appreciate so much."

Frankie helped her into her car, "By the way, where's Timmy?"

"Oh, he's at home with his nurse, Malcolm. I guess I can be thankful they did provide us with that little bit of help."

As she backed out of the space and drove out of sight, Frankie made his way back to April. She was holding on to the paper Joyce had handed her, the wheels in her head turning. Something was adding up but she wasn't sure what it was yet.

"What did you make of all that, a little unusual to find her here, Frankie?"

Frankie nodded. "Definitely too much of a coincidence to ignore, especially seeing as we know this company is connected to four arsons."

April frowned. "Great, the rabbit hole just keeps getting deeper, lets question the assistant and get out of here, I got a feeling this is far from our last stop."

***

It was almost dinner time when April returned Frankie to his home. The conversation with the assistant didn't yield any results. To make things worse, even though councilman Nash tried to help, Nash Developments' lawyers demanded a court order before they'd turn over any documents. Of course, they wouldn't be able to get one until morning which meant that part of the investigation came to a screeching halt.

Joyce did deliver on a mountain of paperwork: memos from different companies and news reports from different cities where Nash Developments had properties. April had said it would take her all night to comb through it for anything worthwhile. Frankie offered to assist but April reminded him he had a family to get back to and this wasn't his job.

As he put his gun away and sat in his favourite chair, he pulled the badge from his side and stared at it. He laughed, thinking of all the times he had made fun of officers, for being the second best, or being too dumb to know how fire, works. Now he was acting like one but doing this meant he could help end this madness. He thought back to the fire the night before, to hearing the explosion and hearing Sammy scream in pain.

"Daddy why are you crying?" Young Franklin's voice broke his trance, he hadn't even noticed he had tears in his eyes. He reached down and picked up his son and held him close.

"Daddy just had a hard day, son but it's all better now."

Chapter 11

Captain Cline always kept odd hours, so it was normal to see him in the office at night. He had been researching properties throughout the county files trying to find any that may be next on the arsonist hit list. So far, he had stumbled on five likely targets, all formerly owned by Fishburn Property Management Corp.

Two of the properties operated twenty-four hours and had security on site, which made him think they would be less than attractive as potential targets. The third was almost two hundred acres of land outside of town that was being discussed for a major development but there was nothing there but trees. This left him with an old gas station and restaurant on the Old Lake Highway and a small manufacturing facility on the far side of the county.

Geographically, the gas station was the most likely, so he decided that would be the best bet. He grabbed his keys and badge, holstered his duty weapon and left the office.

It was a fifteen-minute drive out to the station. It was almost midnight and the road was dark, with almost no one on it this late at night. He could see the moon reflecting off the lake to his right as he passed close to the water.

He pulled into the parking lot in front of the abandoned building and called his location in to dispatch. He started checking the front doors and windows, most of them covered with old ads and signage. The store's shelves were still there, only bare of any goods. The restaurant had several booths he could see but the rest of the floor was clear and in some part of renovation, before the previous owner was bought out.

He went around the side of the building. There was a small access road that went back to an old boat landing, probably the main source of customers in this remote location. There was even a blue van parked down the road away, undoubtedly kids thinking they'd found a safe place for making out. He decided he'd finish checking the building before he told them to move on. As he made his way to the back of the building, he noticed an open door.

"Dispatch this is County 46 be advised I have an open door, send me a unit to help clear the building," he said into his radio.

There was a brief reply of acknowledgement and the captain decided to ready his weapon just in case. He moved to the other side of the door and continued down the wall to the next corner and peered around the side. He noticed a second door to the back of the restaurant but he couldn't tell if it had been opened. He started back around the way he came to cover the front of the building until back-up arrived.

He caught movement out of the corner of his eye, only a glimpse. He turned, trying to bring his weapon to bear on the target but it was too late. A shot rang out as a person came fully into his line of sight, slender with a hood covering their head. He couldn't see a face as the bullet ripped through his torso. He stumbled back, his pistol falling from his hand as the second shot was fired.

Captain Cline felt the second bullet tear through his shoulder as he fell to the ground. His attacker ran off towards the van he had ignored earlier. He could make out only the slender figure in blue jeans, a hoodie and white sneakers running. Suddenly, there was a loud noise and bright flash behind him but he couldn't turn to see what it was. He was struggling to remain conscious as his eyes clouded.

The last thing he remembered was the sudden warmth on his back, as the world faded into black.

***

"Come on, tell me who the lucky guy is," Scott whined, as he drove Medic 12 along Old Lake Highway back towards the station. They were working an overtime shift so the team that regularly worked the unit could take a much-needed vacation. It was after midnight and they had just cleared from a frequent flyer call and after attaching a catheter, Kayla was not in the mood.

"There is no guy, Scott. Will you please stop asking?" she grumbled from the passenger seat.

Scott shook his head. "I don't believe you, you've been happier, you cooked Italian tonight and I heard you humming."

Kayla sighed. "I could just be in a good mood you know… it is possible. You act like just because I'm happy and I hum it's because of a guy."

Scott laughed, "Well, you could be in a good mood but then why do you keep checking your phone? Hmmmm?"

Kayla looked at her cell phone in her hand and quickly placed it in her pocket. "There is no guy, Scott."

Scott opened his mouth to rebuke but the radio interrupted him. "Medic 12 what's your location?"

Kayla grabbed the mic, "Thank God, saved by Dispatch" s he, keyed the mic, "Dispatch Medic 12 Old Lake Highway en route back to Medic 12 Station."

There was a pause as they waited to find out if they were going to get a call. After a minute, Kayla keys up again. "Dispatch did you copy my last?"

The radio responded, "Copy Medic 12 need you to respond to gunshot wound 1847 Old Lake Highway, repeat respond GSW 1847 Old Lake Highway PD is on scene."

Scott looked over at Kayla and flicked the switches to activate the lights as he made a U-turn to go back towards the address. "We're on it."

Kayla keyed the mic, "Copy dispatch Medic 12 responding GSW 1847 Old Lake Highway, ETA three minutes."

The radio replied, "Copy Medic 12 be advised signal 4, attempting to get information on Medicare."

Scott's face went pale. "She just said signal 4, that means officer down, right?"

Kayla nodded, "Punch it Scott, this is bad."

As Scott pushed the accelerator to the floor, the radio began to tone out, "Station 22, Station 21, Station 7, Medic 9 respond Structure fire 1847 Old Lake Highway, repeat Station 22, Station 21, Station 7, Medic 9 respond Structure fire 1847 Old Lake Highway."

"That's the same address we're going to, what the fuck?" Kayla said, holding on as Scott took a curve a little too fast.

"I don't know, but three stations, means it's pretty bad," Scott said, as he hit another switch and the siren began to whine through the night.

In less than three minutes, the scene came into view. The building that was once a gas station was now a blazing inferno. In the parking lot were several police cruisers and one unmarked car. A single officer was standing in the road, flagging down the ambulance and pointing towards the side and back of the building.

Kayla leapt from the unit and walked to the side door, grabbing an equipment bag before following the officer. Scott went to the back of the unit and grabbed the stretcher before following behind them. They had to stay back from the building as the heat was becoming intense. As Kayla rounded the corner and came upon the patient, she recognised him immediately.

"Omg, Raymond!" she exclaimed, before tossing the bag down and beginning to assess the patient.

Scott began cutting the shirt off, assessing from the other side. "Raymond? You know him?"

Kayla was checking his pulse. "He's Sylvia's stepfather, he's raised her since she was five."

Scott nodded. "Not important now, breathing is shallow."

Kayla started to cut away his shirt. "Pulse is weak, Raymond, Raymond can you hear me." Captain Cline did not respond. "He's unresponsive." She was careful not to damage the areas of the shirt where the bullets went through as she removed it, revealing his injuries.

"We need to get him loaded. I'm gonna check on the bird and find out where we can meet them," Scott said, as Kayla began to apply dressings to the entry wounds.

Kayla began setting up oxygen for the patient as Scott returned, positioning the stretcher, "We have to transport, a storm's coming in and Medicare is grounded."

Kayla looked up at one of the officers. "First truck that gets here we need a driver and we need to go asap."

The officer nodded and ran towards the street to wait for a truck. The other officer helped Kayla and Scott put the captain on the stretcher. Kayla strapped him in and secured the oxygen mask to his face, before starting to push it towards the truck.

As they rounded the front of the building where the ambulance was, a firefighter from engine 221 came and helped; others were already spraying water on the fire. He grabbed the bag from Kayla and helped them lift the stretcher into the back.

"I'll try to give you as smooth a ride as possible guys, PD said they're gonna try and escort us." Once Scott and Kayla climbed into the back, he shut the door and proceeded to leave the scene preceded by a police cruiser.

Chapter 12

Kayla and Scott and began moving as if guided by instinct. As Kayla attached the various monitors and wires to the patient, Scott began prepping a saline bag. Without hesitation, he slid a large bore needle into his arm and connected the tubes, allowing the liquid to flow freely.

"Normal saline running wide open, what's his BP?" Scott said, making a note on a strip of paper before reaching for a vial of medication.

Kayla looked at the screen as she finished connecting the wires to their twelve lead EKG, "I'm showing ninety over thirty, we need to check for tension pneumothorax."

Scott grabbed his stethoscope and began to listen to his lungs on his affected side. He couldn't hear anything. He looked and noticed his trachea had shifted to the right, away from where his chest was hit.

"Shit Kayla, his trachea is already shifted, we need to decompress now," Scott exclaimed.

Kayla grabbed a large needle and began to feel along the captain's rib cage, judging the space between the bones. She connected the needle to a large syringe and removed the stopper. She found her mark between the second and third rib and stabbed the needle into his chest, relieving the pressure in the intercostal space. Air mixed with a little blood came gushing out.

Satisfied she had stabilised his air way, she began noting the reading she was getting from the equipment. She grabbed the radio mic and switched to the encode channel.

"Medu ER this is Medic 12 on encode" she said.

There was a brief pause then a voice replied, "Medic 12 go ahead."

"Medu ER, we are inbound to your facility, with an approximately late forties male, GSW to the right thoracic chest wall, exit wound below the ribs two inches from the spine, secondary GSW to the left shoulder. Patient is unconscious, on O_2 at fifteen litres per minute via face mask. BP is ninety over thirty, pulse is thirty-five respirations seven and ragged. Patient has been treated for tension pneumothorax. We have established IV access at this time with eighteen gauge running saline wide open."

"Medic 12 copy, notifying trauma surgeons, monitor breathing and administer meds as per protocol."

"Medic 12 copies, be advised this is a signal 4."

The was a longer than usual pause and the radio finally responded, "Medu copies Signal 4."

Scott was prepping a vial of morphine to add to the IV when the EKG started to beep loudly. "He's tachy, we may need to shock him," he said, dropping what he was doing and grabbing the automatic external defibrillator.

Kayla grabbed the pads from Scott and began to place them on the captain's chest. Scott turned the machine on and there was a high-pitched whirr. After a few seconds, the machine began to beep several times, followed by it saying loudly, "Shock advised, shock advised."

Scott yelled, "Clear," and Kayla threw her hands in the air. A push of a button sent two hundred joules of electricity surging through the captain's body. The EKG continued to beep a long tone. Kayla placed her hand on his chest and began to give compressions until the machine again called out, "Shock advised, shock advised."

Scot yelled, "Clear!" once more and as soon as Kayla was clear, he again pressed the button. For a moment, they both held their breath waiting to see if the captain's rhythm would stabilise. The long tone quit and a steady rhythmic beep took its place. Kayla began checking the other vitals.

"He's stabilised for now. Push a round of Epi and then the lidocaine," she said, grabbing the mic, "Medu ER, Medic 12."

"Medic 12, go ahead."

Medu, be advised — patient became tachycardic, administered shock times two, patient has stable rhythm, we are running first line cardiac and lidocaine."

"Copy Medic 12, what's your ETA?"

"Medu, ETA is five minutes."

Kayla turned back to her patient. Scott was checking the wound on the shoulder to see if the quick clot had worked. His breathing seemed more stable and when she looked, his oxygen saturation was at ninety-five, barely passing but much better than before. Raymond let out a small groan, the first sound he'd made since they'd arrived on scene.

"That's a good sign, right?" Scott asked, "I mean, he's stabilising so we're on the right track here."

Kalya placed her hand on Raymond's arm. "Mr. Cline, can you hear me, it's Kayla."

Again, Raymond let out a groan and uttered a single word, "Sylvia," before falling silent again.

Scott looked at the monitor then back to Kayla who obviously was deeply concerned. "Hey, he's still fighting and he just said his daughter's name. I mean, that's gotta show some good cognitive response."

Kayla nodded, "When I talked to her earlier, she had told me they had been fighting. She probably doesn't even know yet."

The ambulance turned into the hospital's emergency department. Kayla and Scott began moving equipment to rest on the stretcher so they could move Raymond. The doors swung open and their firefighter driver and the officer who had escorted, began helping them offload. As they made their way to the door, a team of nurses were waiting.

"We're setting him up in trauma bay two," The lead nurse said, grabbing the front of the stretcher and guiding it. Kayla gave a full rundown of everything that she knew. She explained every treatment she and Scott had applied as they began switching their equipment for the hospital's equipment. For every wire she disconnected, a nurse would be replacing one of theirs.

Eventually, they transferred care completely and stood outside of the trauma bay for a brief moment, with their stretcher now only holding equipment. They watched as the doctors and nurses went to work at their craft. It was less than a minute before the surgical team arrived to take him into an operating room.

Scott glanced at the worried faces around him and sighed, "I'm gonna get started on the report, you wanna put the truck back together?"

Kayla nodded. "I'm on it. I have to call Sylvia and let her know what's going on."

The officer spoke up. "Ma'am, if you want, I can go and get her. It might be best instead of letting her drive herself."

Kayla nodded in agreement and he rushed out the door. The firefighter gave her a knowing look, grabbed the stretcher from her and nodded as he went out to start helping with cleaning the ambulance.

Kayla made her way to the staff break room. Normally when

she was in here it was to gossip with the nurses. With a major trauma in the ER, it was empty at the moment. She pulled her cellphone out of her pocket and looked at it. Less than an hour ago she didn't want to put it down, now she wished it didn't exist.

She pulled up her recent call list and dialled the last number she had called. There was a moment of silence and then it began to ring. On the third ring it was answered.

"Hey beautiful, took you long enough," a voice said on the other end.

Kayla exhaled and her voice almost broke as she spoke, "Sylvia, get dressed honey and hurry."

Chapter 13

Wayne awoke to the sound of his phone ringing. It was dark in the room and he had to fumble around to find it.

"Hello," he answered groggily. For some twenty years he had been receiving calls in the middle of the night, yet it never got any easier. Crystal sat up next to him. Over the years, she'd come to learn these types of calls were never good. She had got used to the groggy way he'd answer, followed shortly by him jumping off the bed, throwing on clothes and running out the door.

Wayne was silent for a second, nodding, then suddenly his face changed. "Why the fuck didn't you lead with that, Scott?"

Crystal wasn't used to that reaction. In fact, Scott usually gave direct and clear information. Wayne began grabbing his clothes. Crystal rushed to help him gather his things, bringing him his boots and a clean shirt.

"What hospital did they take him to?" Wayne said, as he slid into the shirt his wife held.

She grabbed his keys and wallet from the dresser as he began sliding on his socks and boots. She could only imagine what could've happened. Was Frankie in a wreck? Did Watts date a crazy woman who stabbed him again? Had someone been hurt in a fire?

"I'm already dressed damn it, just don't go anywhere until I get there." He hung up the phone and turned to his wife, taking a deep breath before speaking.

"The arsonist struck again, baby. He set fire to the old station on Old Lake Highway where I used to take Adam fishing."

Crystal reached out for him. Something was wrong, "What else happened? You wouldn't be this upset if it was just a fire."

Wayne shook his head. "One of the detectives on the case was out there. I don't know why but the detective was shot."

"Oh my God!" Crystal covered her mouth, her eyes filled with fear of the knowledge of what that could mean. "Is he...?"

Wayne kissed her forehead. "I don't know yet but I'm on my way to find out."

The rain was just starting as Wayne pulled out of his driveway. The lightning flashes lit up the dark road way as if it were day. It was as if the storm outside was mirroring the storm he was feeling within.

The wet roads and lowered visibility from rain made him drive slower than he wanted to. Twice he swerved to avoid debris the storm had knocked into the roadway. After twenty minutes he reached the hospital and found a place to park that wasn't too far from the emergency entrance.

He made his way to where the ambulances were parked. Medic 12 was still on the pad, parked next to Medic 9, a firefighter in the back trying to put it back together. Wayne used the emergency code to open the door and made his way to the Emergency Medical Service room.

Scott and two other medics were sitting pouring over paperwork. The atmosphere of the room was one of despair and sorrow. Wayne wasn't happy with the silence and immediately decided to break it.

"What's Medic 9 doing here?" he asked, standing in the doorway. His voice startled everyone in the room and for a moment, they were all stunned to see him.

Scott cleared his throat before answering, "Sorry boss, they got here after I called, one of the guys on from Station 22 twisted his ankle out there on the scene. Everything else out there is under control though."

Wayne nodded. "Where's your partner?" He looked again to see if he could find Kayla at the nurse's station or anywhere visible.

Scott looked down at the report he was finishing. "Cap, she's close to this one man, it turns out she and Sylvia are umm." He stopped short of confirming what he suspected. She hadn't admitted it but the minute Kayla realised who it was, it was obvious she was involved somehow.

Wayne got frustrated with Scott beating around the bush; his lieutenant should know better.

"Out with it, Mellon, what is the situation?" he growled.

Scott took a breath. "I think she's dating Sylvia and apparently the detective was Sylvia's step-dad. They're in the family waiting room with a couple of officers. Sylvia didn't take it very well."

"You saw the injuries. How bad was it really?"

Scott shook his head, "Fifty / fifty boss, he took a hit through the bottom of his chest cavity and out the back, close to the spine; it probably hit everything in between. He actually coded once on the way in but we got him back, even stabilised his rhythm but that kind of damage, who knows? I'll say this much, he's a fighter and you and I both know how important that is."

Wayne nodded and began to turn away. "Get those units squared away and back in service. I'm gonna see if you need a replacement partner."

He left the EMS room and crossed over to the nurses' station, before making his way to the surgical waiting area. He paused near a vending machine area when he heard a familiar voice talking. He was almost sure it was Frankie asking questions.

"So, as you were approaching the scene you saw a minivan heading past you at a high rate of speed. Did you remember anything about the driver?" Frankie was questioning an officer in front of the coffee machine.

"Uh, yeah, blue van and the driver had on a hoodie so I couldn't make out much, white maybe small-framed, for sure."

Wayne stopped and watched for a moment as the officer was in thought. He couldn't figure out why Frankie was asking him questions. Then he saw the badge on his belt. Frankie was moonlighting. *'I'm gonna kill him,'* Wayne thought. He was about to approach them when he remembered that Kayla may need him more right now. Wayne made a mental note to deal with this insubordination later and continued on his way.

As he turned the corner into the waiting area, he found Sylvia and Kayla sitting on chairs along the wall, nearest to the door to the surgical ward. Kayla was trying to comfort the young, red head and didn't even notice Wayne approaching them. Wayne sat down across from them and leaned forward, arms resting on his knees and cleared his throat.

The noise startled both women, who had assumed they were alone. Kayla had been keeping the relationship a secret and the realisation that her captain now knew, seemed to overpower the knowledge that he was also her friend. Sylvia had also not wanted anyone to find out and being face to face with the next assistant made her pale skin even paler. Wayne shook his head as he wondered if he was really that much of a hard ass.

He spoke softly, trying to convey kindness for the young woman. "How are you holding up, kid?"

Sylvia sniffled a little. "I'm doing my best captain. Sorry I didn't notice you come in."

Wayne shook his head. "There's no rank in here right now, I just want to make sure you're okay. I never knew your dad was a cop."

Sylvia gave a shy smile. "Well, you know the whole FD versus PD thing. He married my mom when I was really little and he's always been there for me."

Wayne nodded. "That doesn't matter when it comes to family; we're all here for you."

Sylvia nodded and reached up to wipe a tear away while still holding Kayla's hand. Kayla looked at Wayne, expecting him to say something but he seemed unphased. He glanced over at the door and then back at the two women.

"Have there been any updates since they took him back?"

"I haven't seen anyone yet. I wouldn't know anything if Kayla hadn't told me what she knew."

Wayne frowned and furrowed his brow. "Kayla, do you want me to call in another medic to finish out the shift?"

Kayla looked at Sylvia, who gave her an encouraging nod. "No, sir, I'll go back on the truck and finish it out, thank you though. Are you gonna be here with Sylvia so she's not alone?"

"Well, technically there's about five officers I've seen around here, among other people but yeah, I'm not going anywhere."

He stood up and started towards the vending machines. "I'll give you two a minute, I need a water. You want anything, kid?"

Sylvia shook her head. "No, thank you, sir."

He left them and made his way to the vending machines. Frankie had already left. Something he would deal with later. He selected a bottle of water and began to look at the candy machine when he heard footsteps behind him.

"Wayne, thanks for not making that weird," Kayla said, as he turned around.

"She's a good kid and it explains why you've been so happy. I'll just have to locate the paperwork that you filed to let the department know you've initiated a romantic relationship, because I know you followed the department's regulations right."

Kayla smiled and hugged him. "It'll be there I promise, thank you." She gave him a kiss on the cheek and walked away. Wayne chuckled to himself. Sometimes he really did feel like he was the only grown up in the group.

Chapter 14

Wayne waited with Sylvia for several hours before they received any word. During that time, the room slowly filled up with officers and friends. Barry, David and Chief Rose came together, an hour after Wayne had got there. Even the Sheriff himself arrived eventually. They all came and spoke briefly with Sylvia and proceeded to go and talk amongst themselves.

Wayne stayed by Sylvia's side, knowing that would be what Kayla wanted. He didn't yield his post, even when David offered as he was her superior. Instead, David took a seat next to them and waited with them, watching the clock as it slowly ticked on into the night.

It was just after 4:00 a.m. when a doctor finally emerged from the surgical ward. He searched the room for Sylvia, finally noticing her small frame amongst the crowd. He came and asked her to come with him. Wayne, of course, accompanied them, mouthing to David to call a chaplain, just in case.

They were led to the ICU and the doctor stopped outside the door. He looked down for a moment wringing his hands.

"Miss, we've done everything we can for your father. At this point, it's on him to heal. When he arrived, he had massive trauma to his left lung, a lot of internal bleeding, as well as losing a lot of blood. The medics did an excellent job getting him here and he's a fighter but it's now up to him to pull through."

He looked back over his shoulder. "He's still unconscious and he might stay that way for a while but he might wake up at any time. We have him on morphine, his vitals are all stable at the moment. We just need him to wake up. I thought you'd want to see him. Sometimes when a loved one is near, it helps encourage a patient to wake up."

Sylvia fought back the tears she had welled up and simply nodded. She looked back at Wayne who gave her a quiet nod. She used the sleeve of her shirt to wipe her eyes and followed the doctor through the door.

Wayne leaned against the wall across from the door to wait. He wasn't sure how long she'd be but he wasn't going to abandon her now.

***

It took almost a half hour before Sylvia returned from her stepfather's side. Wayne accompanied her to the ICU waiting room and stayed until Kayla arrived, later that morning. It had been a long night but he knew this was far from over.

Wayne made his way to the county headquarters; he knew there would be turmoil when he got there. An officer lay clinging to life and someone had to answer for that. The sheriff would want answers, the council would want answers and right now, he wanted answers. He was tired of being a day late and a dollar short.

He parked his truck in his father's old parking space and looked at the name plate that had yet to be removed. All he had to do was say yes and they wouldn't have to change a thing, because it would still belong to Assistant Chief Miller. He wasn't normally one to make things easy for people but this would have to be an exception he figured.

He made his way into the office building and headed for the

chief's office. He knew from experience that right now, the sheriff and probably Councilman Nash were there pointing fingers and placing blame. He had seen his father during situations like this before, smoothly navigating the turbulent waters that politics and interdepartmental work required.

"You allowed a firefighter to join the investigation and then didn't make sure that all information was being shared," Councilman Nash barked out violently.

Wayne walked in, expecting to have to defend the chief but it was the sheriff who was on the defensive. "I allowed a certified and trained responder with experience in the field of investigation to join my reserve unit. This is very common and might I remind you, allows me to supplement manpower that has been limited by the council."

Wayne looked at Chief Rose for guidance as to speak. The chief shook his head and simply watched the two men squaring off.

"Why don't you explain why your lead detective went to a potential crime scene without backup or wearing proper safety gear?"

"He advised dispatch he was looking at the property and the second he saw something was amiss, he called for backup. Check the tapes before you make accusations."

Councilman Nash had clearly hit a nerve and he knew it, so he turned his attention to Chief Rose. "We need to make a statement to the public. Who is going to do that and what exactly are you going to say?"

Chief Rose looked across his desk at Wayne and gave a slight grin. Wayne nodded. "Well, Mr. Nash, after I collect my new badge, I intend to meet with the detective and the Fire Marshal to arrange to make a media statement. Now, we would like that statement to reflect the cooperation and assistance you have given this investigation, unless you think that's a bad idea."

The sheriff and Councilman Nash just stared at him in shock for a moment. Eventually, the councilman nodded his head. "Well, that sounds like it works, gentlemen. I'll leave you to it," and he slowly made his way from the office.

The sheriff shook his head. "Did you just wing that? Like that was the best line of bullshit I've heard ever and I played poker with your father."

Chief Rose: "So you're taking the job then, congratulations Assistant Chief."

Wayne nodded. "Dad always said you needed backup in situations like this and I couldn't, in good conscience, let either of us deal with much more of that."

The sheriff began to laugh heartily and Chief Rose chuckled as he slid a small box across the desk to Wayne. "I knew you'd come around, so I had these ordered for you."

Inside were a set of brass Assistant Chief bars, a nameplate and an Assistant Chief's badge. Wayne went to say thank you when he placed a second box on the desk. "This should be the first thing you hang in your new office."

Wayne opened the box and inside was a plaque. It read '*In memory of William Miller — Assistant Chief*'. On the plaque was his father's badge and sheriff's office badge, the department patch and the assistant chief bars. Wayne looked over at the sheriff slightly confused but the sheriff must have expected his question.

"You remember those midnight raids we used to do? Well, your father was the first tactical medic we ever had. It was his idea and he recommended every medic we ever used. He earned that badge, bub."

Wayne fought back the tears that were forming in the corner of his eyes. He was both happy and terribly sad at the same time. He steadied himself for a moment. "Thank you, both of you, this means a lot."

The sheriff patted him on the back and made his exit. Chief Rose smiled and pointed towards the office neighbouring his. "I doubt you'll ever use it if you're like your old man but that's yours. Now about the firefighter moonlighting without permission."

Wayne thought about what he was going to do about that. Frankie was doing what he thought was right but he didn't get clearance and he was investigating something he was definitely too emotionally involved in. Still, Wayne knew Frankie and he wasn't going to let this go, especially now that someone had been shot.

"Chief, what would my predecessor have done if I had gone off half-cocked on my own," Wayne said, hoping to find wisdom in his father's actions.

Chief Rose laughed. "You mean every time you went off and didn't listen to him? Do you know how many times he recommended you be fired or forced to resign? He loved you being a firefighter but he hated you fighting fire son."

"That sounds like dad all right, he and I always butted heads."

"Wayne, if it wasn't for the councilman being involved, I'd tell you to let it go but you're gonna have to do something; at least to show the department's position."

The department position was that any officer doing emergency service outside of the department had to notify command first. It had something to do with insurance reasons and it was more for working with other departments in the neighbouring counties. It wasn't to prevent anyone from working, it was so the department could track injuries or conditions where a responder might be overworked. Violating the policy was a paperwork issue normally but Wayne thought this time it had to be handled differently.

"Don't worry, chief," Wayne said, walking across the hall. "When he comes on shift tomorrow morning, I have the perfect way to handle it."

Chapter 15

Wayne went to Station 21 the next morning to take care of some things he felt he needed to handle in person. He arrived early and met with Scott, first to inform him he would be acting captain until one could be appointed to the position. He called Detective Wells and told her she needed to meet with him before shift and then he waited.

April and Frankie arrived at almost the same time and Frankie was very surprised to see the detective there. In front of the door to the station, stood Wayne and Scott. Wayne didn't hesitate and approached them both.

"Perfect timing. I want this over with," he said, walking up to them both.

"Hi Wayne, what's going on?" April said, obviously confused.

"Morning Cap," Frankie said, not sure what could be on Wayne's mind.

Wayne nodded. "It's Chief now, and Detective Wells do you want to explain to me why you took a firefighter from my department on a ride, along without advising his commanding officer, or the department in general?"

April didn't know what to say but Frankie wasn't going to let her take the blame herself. "Wayne, I should've told you, man, we just were trying to keep your name out of everything, ya know — plausible deniability and all?"

Wayne looked at Frankie. "So, you violated department and

county policy and you did it on purpose, am I right?"

Frankie shook his head. "Yeah, what the hell man?"

Wayne glanced over at Scott and back at Frankie. "Let me cut this short, because I have to go and give a press conference in thirty minutes. Today is the first day of your paid suspension. Don't let me catch you in this house until you get this out of your system."

April began to speak up in his defence but Wayne cut her off. "You have a job to do, I don't want one more drop of blood spilled because of this asshole, so figure it out."

He turned and stormed off, or at least to them it seemed like he did. Secretly he was laughing. Frankie was shocked and dumbfounded as he watched his best friend get into his car and drive off.

"Scott, what the fuck just happened?"

"Well Frank, if I were to hazard a guess, you are being paid to work with April and now I gotta call in two people to have a full shift."

He left them sitting in the parking lot and returned to the station to tell Kayla she would be taking his place on scene and start fixing his manpower issues.

***

Wayne straightened his tie in the mirror and glanced at his reflection. He'd talked to the press before but only when he was told what he could or couldn't say. As assistant chief, that decision was now his. He had to decide what to tell the press and what he couldn't. He knew if he gave away too much it could inform the arsonist and perhaps make him more dangerous or harder to catch. Still, if he could give out accurate information perhaps someone saw something and could help with the investigation.

He walked out of the bathroom and into the county council chambers, where a small group of reporters had assembled. The sheriff and chief were already there waiting along with a few members of the county council. He stepped up to the small podium and waited for the room to quieten down.

"Good morning, I am Assistant Chief Miller. I'm here today to give you an update on a series of events that occurred over the past seventy-two hours. We will take any questions after I am done, so please hold them until then."

There was a slight murmuring amongst the reporters but no one objected so he continued.

"Over the past several weeks, there have been a series of arsons we now believe may be connected. We made this determination because we believe the same accelerant was used at each fire. The investigation is being conducted by the Lake County Sheriff's Department and the Lake County Fire Marshal and Fire Department are assisting in any way that we can."

"Three nights ago, there was a fire at the propane storage facility. The fire was caused by a faulty electrical wire. However, during the clean up a device set at the scene ignited, injuring a firefighter. At this time, he is in Lake County Hospital in a stable condition. The investigative team believed they had reason to suspect a pattern for the fires the following night and the detective went to investigate a location he thought might be a target. It is believed the investigator surprised the culprit in the act, which resulted in an officer being shot. At this time, the officer is in a critical condition at Lake County Hospital."

"We are currently working with state authorities to identify the suspected culprit in the act. We ask any citizen who may have information pertaining to these events to please come forward. Lake County takes the protection of its citizens and responders very seriously and will continue to keep you abridged of information, as it becomes available to us. At this time, I'd like to turn things over to the sheriff who also has a statement."

Wayne stepped away and the sheriff and chief took over the press conference. He waited for a moment to make sure he wouldn't be missed and quickly made his exit. He had a lot of work to get done today and not all of it could be done in front of cameras.

Wayne walked into his new office and began to take stock for the first time since he'd taken his father's job. In the corner, were several boxes of his father's things that he had kept here over the years. The chief was planning on delivering it to Wayne but wanted him to go through them here and keep the things of his father's he had wanted.

Wayne picked up the plaque the chief had given him and hung it on the wall, before turning to the boxes in the corner. He began sorting the items he found, briefly pausing to enjoy the memories some of the items brought. Memories of times he and his father responded together, or awards he'd been so proud his father had received.

He finally reached the last of the boxes and found a case on the bottom of the pile. It was made of thick, black plastic with a red cross painted on the top. Underneath was the word 'tactical' in thick, white letters. Wayne clicked open the latches and slowly lifted the lid, revealing its contents. A grin spread across his face as he beheld what was inside. "Ah Dad, you knew what I wanted for Christmas."

Chapter 16

April and Frankie decided to make the best of the situation. After a quick trip to Frankie's house for him to change, they proceeded to Captain Cline's office to pick up where he left off. They looked at the files of the buildings he had left out, including the old gas station.

"I can't figure it out. What did he see that made him choose that location instead of the rest of the properties? Was it just a dumb coincidence?" Frankie asked, looking at the file for the Powertech building.

"He had to make some connection between the other fires and that location. I mean, something told him to look there." She had the file for the Jefferies Station in her hands and was thumbing through.

Frankie went to grab another file and a newspaper clipping fell out. "Wonder what this is?" he said, picking it up and he began reading what it said.

"Holy shit, April this is what he found," he said, waving her over. "This is about a bunch of deals Nash development had in the works, to reinvigorate defunct businesses in the area. And it literally lists every single site the arsonist has struck."

April grabbed the clipping and started looking at the map. As she noticed a location on the map, she'd find its name in the article. She continued to read through and saw the few sites named that hadn't had a fire yet. "Frankie, this is a play-by-play list that the arsonist has been using."

Frankie nodded, looking through another file. "Yeah, who wrote the article?"

April looked at the bi-line and her eyes got wide. "Joyce Carson, she's the woman who's been fighting with Nash, right?"

Frankie handed her the file it had fallen out of. "There's no question Nash was responsible for the fire that burned her child and suddenly, she writes that article about how they bought out Fishburn knowing these deals were gonna be on the table."

"She tried to take them out in court, then she tried in the press, so you think now she's trying to do it through fire."

"Look, she's gotta be connected, think about it. She's been around the fire department, she fit the description of the driver seen on Old Lake Highway and she has the van; I think we should at least check her out."

April nodded and grabbed her phone. "Let's see if we can get her to come down voluntarily, then try we'll see what she has to tell us."

***

An hour later, Joyce found herself sitting in a conference room, a cup of coffee in front of her. She sat calmly staring at her phone as she waited. If she was nervous, she didn't show it. Her manicured nails clacked occasionally on the screen as she waited.

April and Frankie entered the room, files in hand and sat across from her. April glanced over at Frankie and nodded for him to take the lead. He smiled and nodded.

"We're sorry to keep you waiting, Joyce, hope it hasn't dragged you away from anything important." He tried to give her a nonchalant smile but it came off as a cheesy grin.

Joyce giggled a little. "My god, you aren't used to

questioning people are you, Frankie? And I'm a reporter. You dragged me to something important I'm sure, I must be close to something to be here."

April's face shifted to a scowl. "Really Miss Carson, you find it amusing to be implicated in the shooting of an officer."

Joyce looked as if she'd been punched in the gut. At first, she couldn't so much as breathe. "You think I shot a cop! Are you crazy? Why would I have done something so horrible? Why would you even think I did?"

Frankie opened the file in front of him and pulled out her news article. "Joyce, you're here because we need to know why you wrote this. More importantly, how did you end up here after your house burnt down in Charlotte and just before the fires started?"

Joyce looked at the article and sighed, "Honestly, did those assholes at Nash put you up to this? I didn't cave when they provided a nurse, so now they try to paint me as a criminal."

She began to gather her things together and Frankie reached across, placing his hand on hers. "Joyce, this is serious. If you really want to help the department, then we need you to help us figure this out."

Joyce stared at Frankie for a minute, their eyes locked in a silent battle. She flinched and sat back down. She placed her phone on the table and opened the recorder. "Can I at least use this for the story later?"

Frankie looked at April who shrugged. "Help us solve this and I don't care what you do with it."

Joyce leaned back in her chair. "Well, to answer your question I was doing a series of pieces about Nash Developments to continue the pressure, to make them own up to their mistakes. I mean yeah, it's not illegal to do what they did but it's still crooked — to buy another company, only because you knew buyers werc coming to the area."

April was confused, "What do you mean by that?"

"Well, I moved down here to my father's old house after Chris died because we had nowhere to go. When I got here, I found out about the Fishburn purchase and that's what my articles were about. Nash knew those properties that had been sitting, were about to have buyers so he dropped a billion dollars to buy Fishburn so they could turn a profit."

Frankie started looking at the list, all of the properties were owned by Fishburn before Nash bought them out. "How did you find out about all of this? I mean where did the information come from?"

Joyce thought for a moment. "Well, a lot of it was research but what got me started was an anonymous file that got mailed to me at the paper, a week after I moved down here."

April cast Frankie a glance. "Can you prove that the information came anonymously?"

Joyce nodded. "Of course, I'm not a rookie journalist, I know you've got to hang on to information like that. It's all in a file at my office."

"Why didn't you come forward with this when the fires started and they matched your story?"

Joyce looked at the two of them, confused. "Who do you think gave that clipping to the other detective? I didn't think to bring him the file but I can give it to you. Didn't he tell you?"

April and Frankie exchanged a look of shock. "When did you give this to the other detective, Joyce?"

"Oh, it was the night of the last fire. I remember that the Propane company had been on the list of quick sales that Nash was trying to do and I came here to see you but you weren't here, so I gave him the information."

April and Frankie followed Joyce to her office. In no time, she produced a file with internal Fishburn and Nash documents. She also handed them a Ziplock baggie that held the envelope. It had no return address but a local postmark.

April looked through the paperwork and started nodding. "So, someone else knew about this before you reported it. That still doesn't explain the van. Where is your van anyway?"

"My van?" Joyce said, not following. "You mean the minivan I drive when I have Timmy. That belongs to his nurse, Malcolm. It was something he got when he took care of his father but he said it's easier to move Timmy in it."

Frankie nodded. "Joyce, what's Malcolm's last name?"

Joyce stopped and thought for a moment. "Umm, it's Gaskins, why do you ask?"

April looked at Frankie. "You don't he's related to that Gaskins, do you?"

Frankie frowned. "I'd bet you a year's salary he is."

"Related to what Gaskins? Seriously, what do you know that I don't?" Joyce said, looking between the two of them.

"Simon Gaskins. He was the silent partner of Ray Fishburn and he died, just before Ray sold the company to Nash and started working for them."

Chapter 17

Malcolm Gaskins always looked up to his father. He was a kind and determined man who tried to use his wealth to help others. Even though Malcolm didn't choose to work in real estate like his father, he felt being a nurse was carrying on that legacy.

They had a special bond, more like best friends than father and son. Malcolm could often be found joining his father for lunch when he wasn't working or enjoying the simple pastime of fishing. The investments in Fishburn Property Management Corp early on, had at one point given them a very comfortable life.

But time is cruel and eventually Malcolm's best friend became his patient. Unable to tend to the needs of the business, Simon turned control fully over to Fishburn. It was during this time that Fishburn began to flounder and as it did, the value of Simon's investment went down.

Malcolm tried to advocate for his father's partial ownership of the company but his complaints fell on death ears. As he watched his father slowly die, so did the business he helped build. It was just after his father's funeral that Ray Fishburn came to Malcolm with a cheque for his father's part of the company at its current value and explained the company was being sold.

His father received less than a quarter of the money he had once invested; most of it went to pay off debts and funeral costs. Simon's will was meant to be generous with a much larger amount being shared. So, after his estate was split between family, Malcolm was left with an old house, and the van he had used to transport his father in.

That was when he discovered what Fishburn had done: taking a deal to work for Nash and receive a cut of the sales of several properties. Money that should have been his fathers was stolen through corporate piracy. He went to Fishburn and threatened to sue but the lawyers informed him he had no legal recourse.

He was dejected as he left the office when he overheard two of the lawyers discussing a reporter who was also suing the company. Security always let him around the office, so it was nothing for him to sneak and find the file. He knew that this woman could win the battle against this company who had stolen his father's legacy.

First, he sent her documents, anonymously of course, hoping she could use them to expose the corrupt processes. When she published the article, he was ecstatic but it didn't do enough. He decided he would go to her and tell her his story.

He showed up at her house on a Thursday. He had never planned on deceiving her but then he saw her struggling with her son. He introduced himself as a nurse and she asked if Fishburn had sent him and he said yes. It was a lie but if he helped her, she would help him — he knew it.

At first her slew of articles seemed to be doing the damage he wanted and he was sure they would cave. They responded with a meagre settlement offer that barely covered what it would cost to send Timmy to the doctors. He couldn't believe the dishonesty of these people who once were so close to his father.

He had to do something. He knew that the first sale was already in progress so he decided to ruin it. He had plenty of supplies that would be considered flammable so he made his way to the church. Within thirty minutes, the building was ablaze and he sat across the street in the shadows, watching as it burned.

The flames excited Malcolm as he watched the old church be reduced to a pile of burnt timbers and ash. He felt vindicated, he was serving justice with red hot flame. A week later, he would do it again only bigger.

The Powertech building didn't burn as well as the church. Most of the building survived the flame and Malcolm barely escaped before responders arrived. He knew he'd have to figure a way to make his next fire bigger and to make it go off when he was safely away.

He spent his free time over the next week experimenting with methods of timing ignition and different mixtures of alcohol for the perfect flame. He suffered a few burns in the process but was more than able to treat them himself. During the day, he would work as a nurse for the reporter caring for her son. He used a few tricks he'd learned to bill Fishburn for his time and any supplies he needed without them realising what he was doing.

Once he had figured out his device, he was ready for his next target. He snuck in with the workers and set everything up in the unused cafeteria, far from where they would be if they were still in the building. He set the timer and left, driving far enough away so he could watch with a set of binoculars and not be seen. When he saw the building collapse his heart filled with glee. Yet again, his vigilante campaign had struck a blow against his enemies.

The next fire had unexpected consequences. He had planned it to go off once everyone had left the building. Something had gone wrong and as a result, someone was injured. For a moment, he considered that he should stop but then he heard the reporter talking. They knew about how the fires were started and they knew someone was targeting Fishburn. It was only a matter of time before he'd be caught.

He was fine with being caught; he was proud of the damage he'd done to Fishburn. But he wasn't done yet. If he was going to pay for his crimes then Fishburn would pay for theirs.

He didn't realise how quickly they would figure out his pattern. He was almost done setting the blaze at the station when the officer arrived. He had parked on the road just behind the building but before he could scurry out the back, the officer was back there. He couldn't be caught, not yet, so he did what he had to do.

He pulled his father's .38 from his jacket pocket and fired twice. Then he ran to his van as quickly as he could and drove away. Not able to enjoy the blaze he had set, troubled him. They had become part of him and he enjoyed watching them grow.

He knew it was too far gone now; he knew he would be caught. He went to work on the final plan — two final fires that would finally satisfy his need for justice. Two more blazes that would bring Fishburn to its knees and let his father rest.

He grinned as he placed the first device on Ray Fishburn's desk. He smiled, walking out of the office greeting the various employees who were part of his father's betrayal. As he passed the security desk, he stopped and spoke to Bruce. After all he was merely a security guard.

"Bruce, you work too hard," he said, fishing a twenty-dollar bill out of his wallet. "Go treat yourself to lunch on me, brother."

Bruce looked at the gift and smiled. "Well, thank you Mr. Gaskins. You know, I guess I could lock the lobby door and go grab a bite."

Malcolm smiled brightly and gave him a little salute as he walked out the door. '*One down and one to go*,' he thought to himself. He watched Bruce lock the door, then walk to his car, passing Ray Fishburn who was on his way into the office.

Malcolm smiled and waved just before climbing into his van.

He was almost done. He knew he was gonna get caught. He knew he was going to go away for what he'd just done. All of his planning and preparation were about to pay off; he only had one stop left. But first he had two small problems he had to deal with.

He looked over his shoulder at Danni and Timmy playing on their Switches in the back. "Hey guys, sorry I had to make you wait. Now let's go get McDonalds."

Chapter 18

Fishburn Property Management Corp offices were ablaze. The parking lot had quickly become triage for the dozen or so employees who had managed to escape or been rescued so far. Wayne pulled his truck in behind Engine 17 and quickly grabbed his medic bag off the top of the case marked tactical. He made his way to command and called to the captain on scene.

"Greg, where do you need me?"

Greg looked over at the patients lying on tarps in the parking lot. "I've got three medic units inbound but if you can help with triage, chief, I'd really appreciate it."

Wayne nodded. "What's the situation inside?"

"I've got two teams inside now on the first floor, one on venting the roof. Wayne, they said it was like a bomb went off in one of the offices."

Wayne nodded. "Okay, get another engine company en route and tell your guys to be careful. If it's our guy, he may have left more than one device."

Wayne ran across to the patients lying on the ground. He was opening his bag when a team exited the building carrying a badly wounded woman. He signalled them to bring her to him.

"Chief, we found her in one of the offices, she must've been right there when it went off."

Wayne nodded and went to work, first placing her on O_2, then setting up a line to run fluids. "Don't worry, we're going to take care of you."

He cut the clothing away from her arms and legs where she was burned the worst and began to wrap them in sterile gauze. He checked to see if any of her vital areas were severely burned but she was lucky. On her face, he applied an ointment to treat the minor burns she'd received from the radiant heat.

Once he was satisfied he had done everything he could for her, here he covered her with a fresh sheet and placed a triage tag next to her that assigned her as high priority. Then he moved to the next patient.

Other medics moved around the triage area going from the more critical patients to those with minor injuries. As the unit arrived, the patients with the highest priority were loaded as quickly as possible. Over the next hour, the three units were able to successfully move all of the patients to the Lake County Hospital ER.

Wayne began packing up his gear when Greg made his way over to him.

"Chief, we need to get the coroner and an investigator out here," Greg said, reaching to help him up.

Wayne looked at the building as firefighters began to exit, pulling the hose out. "How many were there?"

"We found three in the office where the device went off and there were two others in a neighbouring office that we didn't get to in time."

Wayne nodded, pulling his phone from his pocket. "I'll make to call Greg, overhaul the rest of the building and make sure we don't have any hot spots. We'll let David and the coroner have those offices."

Wayne called into dispatch and made the request, then dialled David's office and told him. He made his way to his truck and started loading his bag into the back. He was just about to climb into the truck when his phone rang.

"Chief Miller," he said into the phone, not looking to see who was calling first.

"Baby, I can't get a hold of Danni and she was supposed to be here by now." Crystal's voice came from the other end.

"Honey, we gave her a cell phone that practically never leaves her hand, did you call it?"

"No, I figured I'd call you first and your dad superpowers would work faster, of course I called it," Crystal snapped.

"Okay, okay, dumb question, I know. Where was she?"

"I dropped her off with Joyce to hang out with Timmy this morning and they were supposed to be over here because Jenna and Malik were coming over."

Jenna was Danni's best friend and Danni wouldn't miss hanging out with her for the world; Wayne knew this. "Okay, is Joyce not answering?"

Crystal sighed. He knew that was a dumb question too. "Wayne I can't reach her cell or her house phone; normally if Joyce isn't there the nurse is."

"It's okay I'll use find my phone and locate Danni's phone. I'll call you right back."

Wayne pulled up the app on his phone and began the trace. It only took a few seconds to show the location as being off Old Lake Highway. Wayne knew the area and the only thing out there was the old Raymond Textiles factory and warehouse.

Wayne linked the phone to his truck's Bluetooth, and began to make his way out of the parking lot. He set the GPS in his truck to find the shortest route and headed for Raymond Textiles. He started to call Crystal when Frankie's name showed up on the screen.

"Frankie, look, I'm sorry I gave you the business this

morning bro but I can't talk now; Danni's missing."

"Wayne don't hang up," Frankie yelled through the speakers, "it's Malcolm Gaskins. He was getting his info by posing as a nurse that Fishburn sent to Joyce."

"Frankie, what the hell are you talking about?"

"The arsonist was Joyce's nurse; it was Simon Gaskin's son Malcolm."

Wayne stomped on the gas and put his lights and sirens on. "Frankie, Danni was at Joyce's house and we can't find her."

"What? Joyce is at the sheriff's office helping us with evidence. Have you tracked Danni's phone?"

"It says she's near the old textile factory on Old Lake Highway, get everything over there, I'm on the way."

April yelled over the phone, "Wayne, he's probably armed, don't go charging in there. Let the sheriff's office handle this."

"He's got my kid, damn it. I'm going to kick his ass."

"I will have you arrested, Wayne, I mean it."

"What's that? Can't hear you, sorry bad connection, must be a tunnel," Wayne said before hanging up. He looked down at the speedometer and was doing eighty miles per hour already. He decided to push the gas harder.

He pushed his truck to its limit, driving through the back roads and across fields to cut his time down. Over the radio he could hear tones going out as units were being dispatched to a potential bomb threat. He could hear officers breaking in, advising ETA and staging areas, until they could secure the scene. He took several turns so fast he thought he might roll the truck but he couldn't slow down. He had to get there before something happened to those kids.

The Raymond Textile facility consisted of six buildings of varying size and age. The oldest building, the warehouse, was an old, heavy timber construction of almost ninety years old. It was built along the railroad tracks at the back of the property which ran towards Charleston.

Wayne's shortcut took him to the back of the facility. He jumped the railroad tracks outside the factory and crashed through the back gate by the railroad tracks. He could see the van at the main gate on the other side of the facility, off Old Lake Highway. Wayne sped towards it but knew he couldn't risk hurting the kids. He slid the truck sideways and stopped, just in front of the van. He didn't see anyone in it but the back door was opened.

Wayne jumped out and went to the back of his truck. He grabbed the black case marked tactical that had belonged to his father. Suddenly, the crack of a gunshot echoed as Wayne was hit in the shoulder and spun from the truck.

Malcolm came forward, gun levelled at Wayne. "Just stay down, you can't stop me and I only want to hurt Nash now."

"It's over Malcolm; they're coming for you. Just let the kids go."

"They're too late to stop me. I've already finished off Ray Fishburn; this is just the exclamation point to send a message."

Wayne tried to fight his way up. The pain in his shoulder was intense. "Where's my daughter, asshole?"

Malcolm laughed. "Your kid is smart. She almost stopped all this but you shouldn't worry about her, you should worry about the headache."

Malcolm reared back and smacked Wayne in the head with the butt of the gun. The pain was intense and everything went black.

Chapter 19

Wayne lay unconscious on the ground while Malcolm continued to move boxes from his van into the buildings. He had just left the maintenance shed when he started hearing the sirens getting closer. He could see blue and red flashes approaching. He grabbed one of his boxes and ran towards the old warehouse just as April and Frankie pulled through the main gate.

April started to follow him, when she caught Wayne out the corner of her eye and slammed on the brakes. The car screeched to a halt allowing enough time for Malcolm to duck inside the old warehouse. Frankie jumped out of the car to give chase and then noticed April going the other way.

"What are you doing?" he called to her.

She was running to where the truck and van were parked. "Wayne's down."

Frankie flew past her and leapt across the hood of the truck to the side where Wayne lay, between the vehicles. He grabbed his best friend and began to shake him to get him to respond then he noticed the blood.

"Fuck, he's been shot, grab the coagulant outta his med kit; we gotta stop the bleeding."

April reached in the back of his truck, grabbed his med kit out and handed it to Frankie. "I don't know what that is man, I'm not a medic."

Frankie grumbled momentarily and then reached in. Wayne had set up every responder's medical bag the same to make sure you never had to search for things like this. Frankie grabbed the bag and began applying the chemical to the wound in Wayne's shoulder, stopping the blood flow. He quickly dressed the wound and grabbed Wayne's radio.

"Engine 212, this is Casselman, we have the suspect in the old warehouse, stage on the back side of the facility until we advise the warehouse is clear."

The radio crackled. "Engine 212 copies, all units moving to the back gate for suppression operations."

"Engine 212 I need you and Medic 9 to come to the main gate. We have a Signal 4, at the assistant chief's truck."

The radio was silent but the revving of the engines of the equipment heading towards them was unmistakable. "Engine 212 coming hot."

McMurray didn't brake when he came through the gate, swinging the truck wide to come back and create a barrier between the warehouse and everyone else. It knocked over the gate and part of the fencing in the process. He, Kayla and Scott leapt from the engine and made their way to Frankie. Medic 9 pulled up right by where they were. Watts jumped out and ran to the chief.

"Go finish this you guys, we got the chief," Watts told Frankie, as he began trying to bring Wayne around.

Frankie and April nodded and headed towards the building. They drew their guns and stopped at the main entrance. A few hand signals and a nod, were all they exchanged. Frankie threw the door open and April cleared her line of sight. Frankie followed suit and they disappeared inside.

The medics quickly loaded Wayne onto a stretcher and began to wheel him away. Kayla helped them to load him and as they got fluids in him, he began to regain consciousness.

Immediately he began struggling and trying to get up, practically fighting to get off the stretcher.

"Chief, you gotta calm down, you've been shot," Kayla said, trying to calm him.

Wayne continued to fight. "No, I can't, he's got Danni. I gotta get to her."

Kayla continued to hold on to him. "Wayne, Danni's safe, she got Timmy out and got help, Crystal and the police are with her."

Wayne stopped struggling, his eyes tearing up. "She's okay, right? She's okay."

Kayla patted his head. "She's not gonna be if you kill yourself, let the guys get you to the ER; we got this."

Wayne leaned back. "Kayla, he doesn't want to stop; he's not gonna go down easy. Look in my truck okay, you'll know what to do."

Kayla wanted to ask him what he meant but the medics rushed her out of the truck. As she stood there while they closed the doors, he called to her again, "Check the back of my truck."

Kayla watched as they drove off, then turned and looked at Wayne's truck. The back was still opened and it occurred to her that Wayne must have opened it before he was shot. She made her way to the truck and in the back, she found the black plastic case already unlatched.

Kayla slowly lifted the lid to see what was inside. As she beheld its contents, she realised what Wayne had planned to do from the start. She looked over at Scott, running the scene for a moment, then back to the case.

"Sorry Scott," she said to herself, "Chief gave me new orders."

***

Scott was already setting up attack teams outside several of the buildings. He kept looking back at the medic unit as it started to drive away. He started to make his way to Kayla when an explosion behind brought him back to the reality of the situation.

The closest building erupted in flames. It was the smallest of the six buildings on site, built to mainly house management offices and training classrooms. As flames began to spread from the back part of the building where the device had gone off, Scott began calling out orders to the crew outside.

He called to the engineer on Engine 221, which was set up on that building, "221 set up to run foam, we're dealing with an accelerant, that should help suppress it. Tell them to make entry and proceed to attack with caution. If they see a secondary device, they pull out and we surround and drown."

The engineer responded by blasting his horn once then and the order was executed. Scott looked back for Kayla but he couldn't see her anywhere. He made his way over to the van and looked in the back. There were two boxes in the back of the van. Scott opened one of them and saw it contained another device. He looked at McMurray who was waiting by Engine 212 for the all clear.

"McMurray, we got two devices in this van. Get Wayne's truck clear and then move 212 to a safe location."

McMurray ran to the truck. "I got it LT, where do you want me to stage?"

Scott looked at the warehouse. "We gotta be ready in case that old girl goes."

Scott grabbed his radio and called dispatch. "Dispatch Raymond Command, be advised two of the devices are inside the suspect's vehicle."

"Copy Raymond Command two devices accounted for in the suspect vehicle. Be advised County 49 says the witness saw six devices in the vehicle."

"Copy dispatch, at this time we've had one detonation and crews attempting suppression on the office building at this time. Do you have any word from County 72 of 2115?"

"Raymond Command copied one detonation, be advised negative on any word from County 72, she called for emergency traffic on the channel."

Scott surveyed the scene around him. One building was in flames and five others could catch at any minute. If there were only six devices then he planned one for each building. Scott tried to do the math as best as he could.

The office building was the closest and the smallest. Next to it was the canteen building and the equipment maintenance buildings. They were older structures but mostly open and steel framed. The dye plant was the next building. Abandoned for some time, it was mainly a shell and not much of a threat. Behind that was the main factory, still filled with machines and whatever was left when the old plant closed.

At last, Scott looked at the warehouse; its old structure looming on the furthest part of the facility. It was the oldest building out here, left over from whatever was here before the textile factory. It was heavy timber construction, a method no one really used any more because of its high flammability. Scott knew there was no saving it if a device was set off inside there.

Somewhere inside was the monster who started all of this. He had a device with him most likely and he was in there, with two of Scott's best friends. Scott knew if they didn't stop him, they might not make it out again.

Chapter 20

Inside the warehouse, rows of shelves and crates were spread out throughout the building. Frankie and April moved to cover near the centre aisle and peered around the corner. A few hand signals and they split up, April crossing the aisle and proceeding to the left side of the building and Frankie going to the right.

Frankie reached the end of the first row of shelves and looked down along the side of the building. There had been a lock on the front door that had been cut off, so he assumed Malcolm must still be in the building. He glanced back at April and started making his way up the right side of the building, row by row, checking for any sign of Malcolm Gaskins.

April was following the same style of search on the left side of the building. Thankfully, their training together on Parris Island all those years ago had prepared them. She could look across the building and occasionally get a glimpse of Frankie, as he made the same moves that she would make.

Row by row they searched, looking for any sign of the man or his device. The danger they were in wasn't far from either of their minds. Malcolm was armed and he'd dropped all pretence of trying not to injure anyone. He was mission oriented and if he succeeded, this building would burn around them. If they happened, there was no guarantee anyone would make it out alive.

Frankie held up a balled fist after nearly a dozen rows. This method of searching was the most likely to work but also the most time consuming. As April stopped to look at what he was doing, Frankie tried to think like their quarry. How would he best bring this place down?

The floor of the building was mostly a concrete pad, the wall supports and roof trusses all strong heavy timber; some of it had been replaced during the building's long life. The walls themselves were stucco over what Frankie assumed was wood, outside there was wood panelling. The shelving had been replaced over the years with reinforced steel.

Near the centre of the building was where the older, wooden crates were stored. It was also close to the large, centre structural support. If the fire started there and brought the support down, the entire building would follow. Frankie signalled for April to continue on and he made his way back to the centre of the building.

As Frankie began to approach the crates, a shot echoed through the building. The bullet narrowly missed Frankie's shoulder as he dove for cover a few rows from the building's centre. He couldn't see where it had come from, so he had to hope his partner had not been discovered.

"It's over Malcolm, you're done. Drop the weapon and let's walk out of here," Frankie called out into the building.

There was no reply, only silence answered him. He scanned the rows of shelves for any sign of movement. Unless he located where Malcolm was, he couldn't move without risking being shot.

"Come on, Malcolm, nobody's dead yet." Frankie was counting on Malcolm wanting Fishburn dead. "You've hurt a few people, sure but that's not anything to die over."

"You're lying," Malcolm yelled back. "The only way that bomb would've gone off was if Ray moved it. I may not have got anyone else but I got that bastard."

Frankie was trying to locate him by sound but the echoes in

the place were making it difficult.

"What can I say? Someone got him out and he's already at the hospital, so you've already failed Malcolm, no reason to die here."

April had been making her way along the side of the building, listening to the exchange. When Malcolm answered Frankie, she was almost on top of him. She used his distracted state to sneak up on him. As Frankie lied about Ray Fishburn, Malcolm came into her site.

She took her chance and rushed him, knocking him to the floor and his gun away. She tried to turn and bring her pistol to bear but Malcolm was too fast. Before she could regain her aim, he grabbed a piece of debris and hit her with it, knocking her gun from her hand.

April grabbed him and the two fell onto the ground, grappling for control. April reached for her pistol but Malcolm knocked it away. He struck her across the nose and temporarily dazed her. It gave him the opening he needed. He grabbed the pistol, spun and held it on April as she sat on the floor.

Frankie ran to stop the scuffle but stopped as Malcolm held the pistol on April. "Drop it asshole. I swear I will replace both your fucking eyes before you pull that trigger."

Malcolm grinned. "Counter-offer: you put it down or I'll splatter her head. Like you said, it's over for me, I can't even get my revenge."

They stood frozen, the standoff between them felt like electricity flowing through the air. Frankie felt helpless, Malcolm had nothing to lose and he couldn't close the distance before he pulled the trigger. From behind Malcolm came the sound of a shotgun racking. He spun toward where the sound came from but he wasn't fast enough.

The sound of the shotgun firing echoed through the warehouse. The non-lethal projectile caught Malcom right in the middle of his chest. He was thrown backwards, April's pistol flying from his hand.

Kayla stepped forward from behind the large crates and racked another shell. She was wearing a protective vest and a riot helmet. In her hands, was a modified Mossberg shotgun. She stepped over Malcolm and sneered down at him, "That was for the chief, asshole." Then she reared back and brought the butt of the gun down and across his face. "And that's for scaring one of my babies."

April rushed over and quickly handcuffed Malcolm while Frankie ran up to start looking for the device. Kayla threw down a kitchen timer at his feet and smiled.

Frankie looked down at it and then back up at her. "How long were you in here?"

She giggled. "Long enough to find the device. See, he used the same plan they taught us when we went through that homeland course; and then, to save your ass."

April stood Malcolm up. "What about the other buildings?"

Kayla held up her phone. "I texted Scott what I found; they should be able to disarm the other devices."

They made their way out of the building and were greeted first by several armed officers, pointing   guns at them. As they realised they had the suspect under control, the officer holstered their weapons and began to clap for the trio. As April handed Malcolm off to another officer to read him his rights and take him away, Frankie looked back at Kayla.

"Where the hell did you get all that anyway?" he asked.

Kayla removed the helmet and turned it around so Frankie could read the name '*W. Miller Tach Medic*' stencilled into it.

"I guess the old man still has our back, Frankie."

Epilogue

The headline of the newspaper read:
FISHBURN ARSONIST TO BE SENTENCED MONDAY.

It had been several months since the Raymond fires. The office building was almost completely lost but only one other device detonated and the crews were able to suffocate the fire before it spread too far. So, Malcolm Gaskins didn't get his wish in the end and being caught red handed with a huge amount of evidence, his trail was over quickly.

So much had changed since that day. Captain Cline made a full recovery and much to Sylvia's delight, was home for her birthday. After Sammy recovered from his burns, he went to work with David and Sylvia at the fire marshal's office. April got promoted and received a commendation for her work on the case. Barry decided that it was time for him to retire early and let someone else miss out on time they could be fishing.

Wayne sat the paper on the seat of his truck as he looked up at the activity going on at Station 21. There was still a twinge of pain in his shoulder from where he was shot. It was the last week of June and preparations were being made for the 4th of July celebration on the lake. One thing he would not miss, was all the cleaning that had to be done for celebrations like this.

Wayne made his way into the engine bay and walked around to the side of Engine 212.

"Hey, Probie, come here a minute."

Adam Miller popped his head out from the cab of the truck where he was cleaning. "Yeah Dad, I mean chief; sorry."

Wayne laughed. "You'll figure it out one day. I got a job for you I need done."

Adam jumped out of the truck and stood at attention. "Yes sir, what do you need?"

"Well the Fourth of July parade is this weekend and I believe there's a classic red car out there that is in severe need of a cleaning, if it's gonna ride in it."

Adam grinned wide. "No way, seriously? Hell yeah, thanks Dad." Adam hugged his father who just laughed.

"Probie, what do you think you're doing?" he said.

Adam let go. "Oh yeah, sorry chief, I'll get right on it."

"Not 'til after you got this rig squared away and when you go back to the Academy in two weeks, I expect the best score that place has ever seen."

"Oh, I'm gonna beat your scores by a mile, old man."

Wayne smiled, patting his son's shoulder before turning towards the door to the interior of the station. Watts and McMurray were in the day room cleaning. When he walked in, they smiled and gave Wayne a wave. He turned down the hall to the office, only to find Timmy walking on his crutches, trying to push a dolly with assorted baked goods down the hall."

"Whoa, little guy, what have you got here?"

He smiled up at Wayne. "Mom said I could help out if I was careful. Her and Mrs Crystal were in the kitchen getting things ready, so I'm bringing Mac and Watts a snack."

Wayne looked over his shoulder. "Well, carry on, junior firefighter."

Timmy smiled and squeezed passed Wayne into the day room. Wayne could hear the cheers of Watts and McMurray. He glanced down towards the kitchen to see Joyce, Crystal, Scott and a couple of other firefighters hard at work, trying to make desserts and things for the department's celebration this weekend.

Wayne stopped outside the captain's office and stared at the door. The space where his nameplate once rested was blank. He felt a tinge of longing for the days when this was his office and his team. He knocked on the door three times then waited.

Frankie opened the door and Wayne looked inside. "Oh, you've redecorated," he said, looking around the room, which had a more open flow now. "I don't like it."

The desk now rested in the corner facing the wall. Gone were the filing cabinets and uncomfortable chairs. Instead, there was a comfortable-looking sofa and what looked like it may be a recliner. The walls had different photos but it was still the same people, still the same family. A photo of Sylvia with cake smashed in her face and hair, sat on a small table between the desk and sofa.

Kayla stood smirking. "Well, if you don't like it, you shouldn't have given it to me."

Frankie laughed. "Told you — the second you made her captain this was gonna happen."

"Well, I couldn't just give it to you Frankie, you were coming back off of a paid suspension when Barry decided to retire."

Frankie opened his mouth to retort but stopped short and just shook his head.

"That's what I thought, Lieutenant. If you really wanted the job, you should've out-scored her."

Frankie looked at him with a shocked look. "I'm sorry, didn't she beat your old score by five points on the captain's exam."

Wayne shot Frankie a look and then sat down; it really was a comfortable recliner. "We're not talking about me, anyway that's not why I'm here. As you both know, hurricane season is about to pick up. I know we've done our normal preparations but I want Station 21 to spearhead a program to..."

The tones cut Wayne off as the radio came to life.

"Station 21, Station 7, Medic 9 respond to possible structure fire 4271 Lakeveiw Drive, Station 21, Station 7, Medic 9 respond to possible structure fire 4271 Lakeview Drive, Maps page 17."

Kayla and Frankie grabbed their walkies and started for the door.

"Sorry chief, what was that thing you used to say, Frankie you remember?" Kayla asked, as she walked out.

"Oh yeah. Sorry, can't talk, got work to do," Frankie replied sliding out the door behind her.

Wayne followed them out, watching as firefighters ran out to their units. As he entered the bay, he overheard McMurray shouting,

"Step it up Probie or I'll leave you at the station."

Answered seconds later by, "I'm on, let's roll," and the slamming of the passenger door to Engine 212.

As they made their way on to the streets, lights flashing and sirens wailing, Wayne watched. He stood there watching for just a moment then looked over at his truck.

He ran to his truck and jumped in, throwing on the lights and sirens.

"Fuck this, I'm going too," he said, as he pulled onto the street and joined the responding convoy.

CPSIA information can be obtained
at www.ICGtesting.com
Printed in the USA
LVHW102137170422
716454LV00019B/158

9 781800 741577